SINBAD THE SAILOR
& OTHER STORIES

A TEMPLAR BOOK

Devised and produced by The Templar Company plc
Pippbrook Mill, London Road, Dorking, Surrey RH4 1JE

Illustrations copyright © 1986 by Templar Publishing Ltd
This edition copyright © 1995 by The Templar Company plc

Cover design by Janie Louise Hunt
Designed by Mick McCarthy

ISBN 1-898784-32-9

Printed and bound in Italy

This edition based on *'The Arabian Nights Entertainments'*,
selected and edited by Andrew Lang, originally published by
Longmans, Green and Co. in Great Britain in 1898.

The Arabian Nights

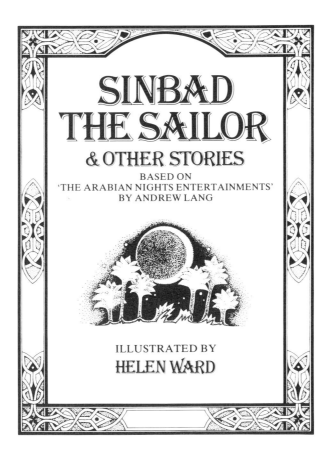

SINBAD THE SAILOR
& OTHER STORIES

BASED ON
'THE ARABIAN NIGHTS ENTERTAINMENTS'
BY ANDREW LANG

ILLUSTRATED BY
HELEN WARD

TEMPLAR

The Arabian Nights', or 'The Thousand and One Nights', are derived from a famous collection of Persian tales which were translated into Arabic in about AD850. They were first introduced into Europe by Antoine Galland, as 'Mille et une Nuits', published between 1704 and 1717, and almost immediately translated into English. There have been countless versions of 'The Arabian Nights', but Andrew Lang's collection, 'The Arabian Nights Entertainments', remains one of the most popular retellings.

Andrew Lang (1844-1912) was a Scottish poet, scholar and folklorist. He is probably best known for his fairy tale collections, the first of which was 'The Blue Fairy Book', published in 1889. 'The Arabian Nights Entertainments', published in 1898, was based on Galland's original version but rewritten by Lang to appeal more directly to children. As Lang remarked in his preface, 'omissions are made of pieces only suitable for Arabs and old gentlemen'.

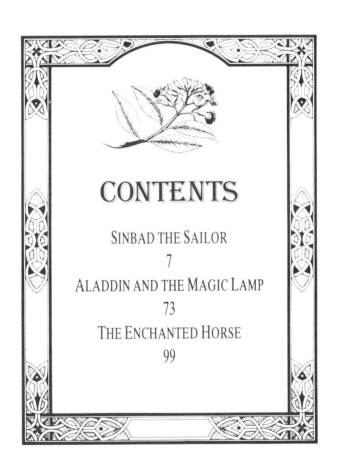

CONTENTS

SINBAD THE SAILOR

7

ALADDIN AND THE MAGIC LAMP

73

THE ENCHANTED HORSE

99

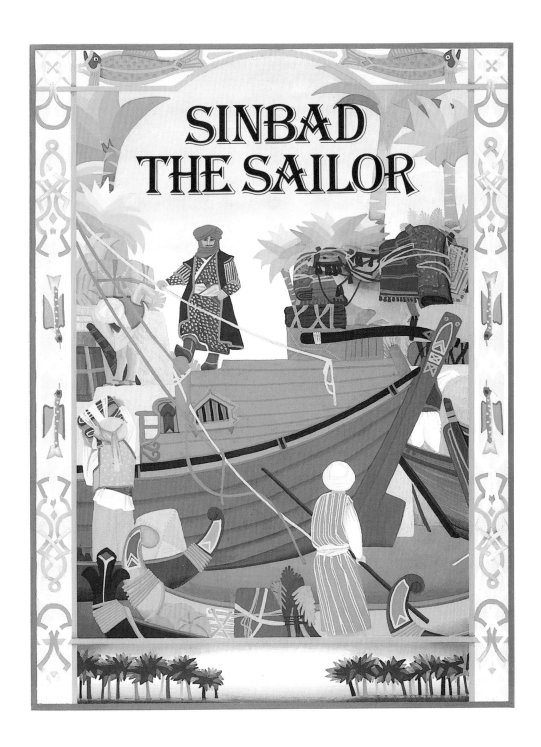

SINBAD
THE SAILOR

n the times of the Caliph Haroun-al-Raschid there lived in Bagdad a poor porter named Hinbad. One very hot day he was sent to carry a heavy load from one end of the city to the other. Before he had gone half the distance he was so tired that he set his burden upon the ground, and sat down to rest in the shade of a grand house. It was a quiet street, the pavement was sprinkled with rose water, and a cool breeze was blowing. Very soon he decided that he could not have chosen a pleasanter place; delicious perfumes came from the open windows and mingled with the scent of the rose water which steamed up from the hot pavement. Within the palace he heard the sound of music and the warble of nightingales, and soon the appetising smell of many dainty dishes reached him also. Obviously a great feast was taking place!

He wondered who lived in this magnificent house which he had never seen before. To satisfy his curiosity he went up to some splendidly dressed servants who stood at the door, and asked one of them the name of the master of the mansion.

'What,' replied he. 'Do you live in Bagdad, and not know that here lives the noble Sinbad the Sailor, that famous traveller who has sailed over every sea upon which the sun shines?'

The porter, who had often heard people speak of the immense wealth of Sinbad, could not help feeling envious of this man whose life was as happy as his own was miserable. Casting his eyes up to the sky he cried out:

'Consider, Lord of all things, the difference between Sinbad's life and mine. Every day I suffer a thousand hardships and misfortunes, and have to work very hard simply to get enough barley bread to keep myself and my family alive, while the lucky Sinbad spends money right and left and lives upon the fat of the land! What has he done that you should give him this pleasant life? What have I done to deserve so hard a fate?'

So saying he stamped upon the ground, beside himself with misery and despair. Just at this moment a servant came out of the palace, and taking him by the arm said, 'Come with me. The noble Sinbad, my master, wishes to speak to you.'

Hinbad was not a little surprised at this summons, and feared that his words might have displeased Sinbad. So he tried to excuse himself, saying that he could not leave the burden which had been entrusted to him to carry. However, the servant promised him that it would be taken care of, and urged him to obey the call so hard that at last the porter agreed.

He followed the servant into a vast room, where a crowd of noble people was seated round a table covered with all sorts of delicacies. In the place of honour sat a tall, grave man with a long white beard. Behind his chair stood many servants, all eager to attend to

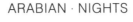

his wants. This was the famous Sinbad himself.

The porter, more than ever alarmed at the sight of so much magnificence, trembled and saluted the nobles. Sinbad made a sign to him to approach and, seating him at his right hand, heaped choice morsels of food upon his plate, and poured him some excellent wine. Hinbad ate and drank his fill, then, as the banquet drew to a close, the great man spoke to him in a friendly way, asking his name.

'My lord,' replied the porter, 'I am called Hinbad.'

'I am glad to see you here,' continued Sinbad, 'but I wish you to tell me what it was that you said just now in the street.'

At this question Hinbad was overcome with shame and, hanging down his head, replied, 'My lord, I confess that, overcome by weariness and bad temper, I said some very foolish words. I pray you to pardon me.'

'Oh!' replied Sinbad, 'do not imagine that I am so unjust as to blame you. I understand your situation and can pity you. Only you appear to be mistaken about me, and I wish to set you right. No doubt you imagine that I have acquired all the wealth and luxury that you see me enjoy without difficulty or danger, but this is far indeed from being the case. I have only reached this happy state after suffering every possible kind of danger for many years.

'Yes, my noble friends,' he continued, addressing the company, 'I assure you that my sea-faring adventures have been strange enough to deter even the most daring men from seeking wealth as I did. You have

probably heard many confused accounts of my seven voyages, and the dangers and wonders I have met with by sea and land, so I would now like to give you a full and true account of them.' And he ordered one of his own servants to deliver the porter's burden, so that Hinbad could stay and listen to the whole tale.

 FIRST VOYAGE

"I had inherited a lot of money from my parents and, being young and foolish, I at first spent it recklessly upon every kind of pleasure. But presently I realized that my money would soon vanish if I managed it so badly, and I remembered also that to be old and poor is misery indeed. So I began to plan how I could make the best of what still remained. I sold all my household goods and joined a company of merchants who traded by sea, leaving from Balsora in a ship which we had fitted out between us.

We set sail and took our course towards the East Indies by the Persian Gulf, having the coast of Persia upon our left and the shores of Arabia Felix upon our right. At first the ship's movement made me very ill, but I soon recovered, and since that hour have never again been plagued by sea-sickness.

From time to time we landed at various islands, where we sold or exchanged our merchandise. Then one day, when the wind dropped suddenly, we found ourselves close to a small island like a green

meadow, which rose only slightly above the surface of the water. Our sails were furled, and the captain gave us permission to land for a while and amuse ourselves. We decided to go ashore, and strolled about for some time, lit a fire and sat down to enjoy our food. But suddenly we were startled by a violent trembling of the island, and those left upon the ship shouted to us to come on board for our lives – since what we had taken for an island was in fact the back of a sleeping whale!

Those who were nearest to the boat threw themselves into it; others sprang into the sea. But before I could save myself, the whale plunged suddenly into the depths of the ocean, leaving me clinging to a piece of the wood which we had brought to make our fire. Meanwhile a breeze had sprung up, the ship's sails were hoisted and, in all the confusion of saving the men clinging to the side of the boat, no one missed me. I was left at the mercy of the waves.

All that day I floated up and down, now beaten this way, now that, and when night fell I despaired for my life. But, weary and exhausted as I was, I clung to my frail support, and great was my joy when the morning light showed that I had drifted against an island.

The cliffs were high and steep but, luckily for me, there were some tree-roots I could grasp and, using them, I eventually managed to climb up. I stretched myself upon the turf at the top, where I lay more dead than alive, till the sun was high in the heavens. By that time I was very hungry, but after some searching I came upon some fruit, and a spring of clear water. Much refreshed I set out to explore the island.

Presently I reached a great plain where a grazing horse was tethered, and as I stood looking at it I heard, from beneath the ground, the sound of voices. A man appeared who asked me how I came upon the island. I told him my adventures, and heard in return that he was one of the grooms of Mihrage, the king of the island, and that each year they came to feed their master's horses that lived on the deserted plain. He took me to a cave deep in the ground where his companions were assembled and, when I had eaten some of their food, they told me how fortunate I was to have come upon them when I did. They were going back to their master tomorrow, and without their aid I would certainly never have found my way out of the wilderness.

Early the next morning we set out and, when we reached the capital, I was kindly received by the king, and told him my adventures. He ordered that I should be well cared for and given everything I needed. Being a merchant I sought out men of my own profession, and particularly those who came from foreign countries. I hoped in this way to hear news from Bagdad, and find out some means of returning, for this capital was situated upon the sea-shore and visited by vessels from all parts of the world. In the meantime, I heard many curious tales and answered many questions about my own country, for I talked willingly with everyone.

Also, to while away the time of waiting, I explored a little island named Cassel, which belonged to King Mihrage, and which was supposed to be inhabited by

a spirit named Deggial. Indeed, the sailors assured me that often the playing of timbals could be heard upon it at night. However, I saw nothing strange upon my voyage, except some giant fish that were a full two hundred cubits long! Fortunately, they were more in dread of us than we were of them, and fled when we struck the boards of the ship to frighten them. There were other fish, too, only a cubit long but with strange heads like owls.

One day after my return, as I went down to the quay, I saw a ship which had just cast anchor and was discharging her cargo. The merchants were busy seeing to it that the goods were removed to their warehouses. Drawing nearer I noticed that my own name was marked upon some of the packages and, after carefully examining them, I felt sure that they were those from my old ship! I then recognised the captain of the vessel but, as I was certain that he believed me to be dead, I went up to him and asked who owned the packages that I was looking at.

'There was on board my ship,' he replied, 'a merchant of Bagdad named Sinbad. One day he and several of my other passengers landed upon what we supposed to be an island, but which was really an enormous whale floating asleep upon the waves. No sooner did it feel the heat of the fire which they had lit upon its back, than it plunged into the depths of the sea. Several of the people who were upon it perished in the waters, and among them was this poor, unlucky man. These goods are his, but I will sell them to help his family if I should ever chance to meet with them.'

'Captain,' said I, 'I am that Sinbad whom you believe to be dead, and these are my possessions!'

When the captain heard these words he cried out in anger, 'Lackaday! and what is the world coming to? In these days there is not an honest man to be met with. Did I not with my own eyes see Sinbad drown, and now you have the cheek to tell me that you are he! You are ready to invent this horrible falsehood to get these goods which don't belong to you!'

'Have patience, and do me the favour to hear my story,' said I.

'Speak then,' replied the captain, 'I will listen.'

So I told him of my escape and of my fortunate meeting with the king's grooms, and how kindly I had been received at the palace. Very soon I began to see that I had made some impression upon him and, after the arrival of some of the other merchants, who showed great joy at once more seeing me alive, he declared that he also recognised me.

He hugged me and exclaimed, 'Heaven be praised that you have escaped from so great a danger. As to your goods, please take them and sell them as you please.'

Of the choicest of my goods I prepared a present for King Mihrage, who was at first amazed, having known that I had lost everything. However, when I had explained the story to him, he accepted my gifts and in return gave me many valuable things.

I then took leave of him and, exchanging my goods for sandal and aloes wood, camphor, nutmegs, cloves, pepper, and ginger, I set sail upon the same vessel.

I traded so successfully upon our voyage home that I arrived in Balsora with about one hundred thousand golden sequins. My family received me with much joy. I bought land and slaves, and built a great house in which I resolved to live happily and forget my past sufferings."

Here Sinbad paused, and commanded the musicians to play once again. The feasting continued until evening and when the time came for the porter to depart, Sinbad gave him a purse containing one hundred sequins. 'Take this, Hinbad, and go home,' he said. 'But come again tomorrow and you shall hear more of my adventures.'

The porter left, quite overcome by so much generosity. As you may imagine, he was well received at home, where his wife and children thanked their lucky stars that he had found such a rich friend.

The next day Hinbad, dressed in his best clothes, returned to the voyager's house, and was received with open arms. As soon as all the guests had arrived, the banquet began as before. And when they had feasted long and merrily, Sinbad addressed them again.

'My friends, I beg that you will give me your attention while I relate the adventures of my second voyage, which you will find even more astonishing than the first.'

 SECOND VOYAGE

had resolved, as you know, on my return from my first voyage, to spend the rest of my days quietly in Bagdad, but very soon I grew tired of such an idle life and longed once more to find myself upon the sea.

So I bought more goods for trading, and set out for the second time in a good ship with other merchants whom I knew to be honourable men. We went from island to island, often making excellent bargains, until one day we landed at a spot which, though covered with fruit trees and many springs of excellent water, appeared to have neither houses nor people. While my companions wandered here and there gathering flowers and fruit I sat down in a shady place and, having heartily enjoyed the food and the wine I had brought with me, I fell asleep, lulled by the murmur of a clear brook which flowed close by.

How long I slept I do not know, but when I opened my eyes and started to my feet, I realised with horror that I was alone and that the ship was gone. I rushed to and fro, with cries of despair, when from the shore I saw the ship under full

sail just disappearing over the horizon. I wished bitterly then that I had been content to stay at home in safety.

But since wishes could do me no good, I took courage and looked about me for a means of escape. I climbed a tall tree and looked anxiously towards the sea but, finding nothing hopeful there, I then turned to look inland. There I was amazed to see a huge dazzling white object, so far off that I could not make out what it was.

Climbing down from the tree, I hastily collected what remained of my food and set off as fast as I could go towards it. As I drew near, I discovered it to be a white ball of immense size and height and, when I could touch it, I found it marvellously smooth and soft. As it was impossible to climb – for there was no foothold – I walked around it seeking some opening, but there was none. I counted, however, that it was at least fifty paces round.

By this time the sun was near setting, but quite suddenly it fell dark, and something like a huge black cloud came overhead. I saw with amazement that it was a bird of extraordinary size which was hovering near. Then I remembered that I had often heard the sailors speak of a wonderful bird called a roc, and it occurred to me that the white object which had so puzzled me must be its egg!

Sure enough the bird settled slowly down upon it, covering it with its wings to keep it warm. I cowered close beside the egg so that one of the bird's feet, which was as large as the trunk of a tree, was just in front of me. Taking off my turban I unwound it and

used the linen to tie myself to one of the bird's feet, hoping that when it took flight next morning, it would bear me away with it from the desolate island. And this was precisely what happened…

As soon as the dawn appeared the bird rose into the air, carrying me up and up till I could no longer see the earth. Then suddenly it descended so swiftly that I almost lost consciousness. When I became aware that the roc had settled and that I was once again upon solid ground, I hastily unbound my turban from its foot and freed myself. It was not a moment too soon! For the bird, pouncing upon a huge snake, killed it with a few blows from its powerful beak and, seizing it, rose into the air once more and soon disappeared from my view. But when I looked about me, I began to doubt if I had gained anything by quitting the desolate island.

The valley in which I found myself was deep and narrow, surrounded by mountains which towered into the clouds, and with sides that were so steep and rocky that there was no way of climbing out. As I wandered about, seeking anxiously for some means of escaping from this trap, I observed that the ground was strewed with diamonds, some of them of an astonishing size. This delighted me – but not for long,

because I also discovered many horrible snakes so long and so large that the smallest of them could have swallowed an elephant with ease. They were hiding in caves deep in the rocks and I realised that – fortunately for me – they only came out by night, probably to avoid their enemy the roc.

All day long I wandered up and down the valley, and when it grew dusk I crept into a little cave and, having blocked up the entrance with a stone, I ate part of my little store of food and lay down to sleep. All through the night the serpents crawled to and fro, hissing horribly, and I could scarcely close my eyes for terror. So I was thankful when the morning light appeared and, when I judged by the silence that the serpents had retreated to their dens, I came trembling out of my cave.

I wandered up and down the valley once more, kicking the diamonds out of my path in contempt. What useless things they were to a man in my situation! At last, overcome with weariness, I sat down upon a rock, but had hardly closed my eyes when I was startled by something which fell to the ground with a thud close beside me.

It was a huge piece of fresh meat and, as I stared at it, several more pieces rolled over the cliffs in different places. In a flash I remembered the stories I had heard sailors tell of the famous valley of diamonds, and I realized exactly what was happening. This valley had many eagles, who made their great nests high up in the rocks. Merchants from Bagdad came to the valley every year, at the time when the eagles were hatching their young. They threw great lumps of meat down onto the valley floor which fell with so much force upon the diamonds that some of the precious stones stuck to them. Then, when the eagles pounced upon the meat and carried it off to their nests to feed their young, the merchants would scare them away with shouts and cries, and would seize the diamonds.

Until this moment I had looked upon the valley as my grave, for I had seen no possibility of getting out of it alive. But now I took courage and began to devise a means of escape. I began by picking up all the largest diamonds I could find, and stored them carefully in my leather wallet which I tied securely to my belt. I then chose the piece of meat which seemed most suited to my purpose and, with the aid of my turban, bound it firmly to my back. This done, I laid face down and awaited the coming of the eagles.

I soon heard the flapping of their mighty wings above me, and felt one of them seize upon my piece of meat, taking me with it. He rose slowly towards his nest and presently dropped me into it. Luckily for me the merchants were on the watch and, setting up their usual cries, they rushed to the nest, scaring away the eagle. They were extremely surprised to discover me there, but also very disappointed at finding no diamonds, so they all began to shout at me for having robbed them of their usual profit. I spoke to the one who seemed most angry.

'I am sure, if you knew all that I have suffered, you would show more kindness towards me and, as for diamonds, I have enough here for you and me and all

your company.' And I showed him the huge, sparkling gems I had gathered. The others all crowded round me in amazement, wondering at my adventures and admiring my escape. They led me to their camp and examined my diamonds, assuring me that in all the years in which they had carried on their trade, they had seen no stones to be compared with them for size and beauty.

I discovered that each merchant chose a particular nest, and took a chance on what he might find there. So I begged the one who owned the nest to which I had been carried to take as much as he would of my treasure. But he contented himself with one stone, by no means the largest, and assured me that with such a gem his fortune was made and he need toil no more. I stayed with the merchants several days and was glad when they asked me to accompany them on their journey home.

Our way lay across high mountains infested with frightful serpents, but luck was with us, and we escaped them to come at last to the seashore. Thence we sailed for Bagdad, stopping awhile at the isle of Roha, where the camphor trees grow to such a size that a hundred men could shelter under one of them with ease.

O n this island we saw a rhinoceros, an animal which is smaller than an elephant and larger than a buffalo. It had one horn about a cubit long which had traced upon it the figure of a man. While we were watching, the rhinoceros had a terrible fight with a huge elephant. Despite his smaller size, he

speared him with his horn and started to carry him off upon his head. Suddenly he was blinded with the blood of his enemy, and fell helpless to the ground. Then along came a giant roc, and clutched them both up in his talons to feed his hungry young. Many other astonishing tales I could tell about this island – but one day you may go to Roha and see for yourselves.

Before we left, I exchanged one of my diamonds for many goods, and traded most profitably all the way home. At last we reached Bagdad, where I gave away some of my money to the poor, after which I settled down to enjoy the riches I had gained with so much toil and pain."

Having told the adventures of his second voyage, Sinbad again bestowed a hundred sequins upon Hinbad, inviting him to come again on the following day to hear the adventures of his third voyage. The other guests also departed to their homes, but all returned at the same hour next day, including the porter whose former life of hard work and poverty had already begun to seem like a bad dream. Once more, after the feast was over, Sinbad began his story – the third of his wonderful voyages.

THIRD VOYAGE

"After a very short time the pleasant easy life I led made me quite forget the perils of my two voyages. And, as I was still in the prime of life, I longed for further adventure. So once more

providing myself with the rarest and choicest goods of Bagdad, I set sail from Balsora with other merchants, heading for distant lands. We had landed at many ports and made much profit, when one day upon the open sea we were caught by a terrible wind which blew us completely off course. It lasted for several days and finally drove us into harbour on a strange island.

'I would rather have come to anchor anywhere than here,' muttered our captain. 'This island and all adjoining it are inhabited by hairy savages, who are certain to attack us. Whatever these dwarfs may do we dare not resist, since they swarm like locusts and, if we hurt one of them, the rest will fall upon us and finish us all.'

These words caused great fear among all the ship's company, and only too soon we were to find out that the captain spoke the truth. For there appeared a vast horde of hideous savages, not more than two feet high and covered with reddish fur. Throwing themselves into the waves, they surrounded our vessel. Then, chattering in a language we could not understand and clutching at ropes and gangways, they swarmed up the ship's side with such speed and agility that they almost seemed to fly.

You may imagine the rage and terror that seized us as we watched them, neither daring to hinder them nor able to speak a word to deter them from their purpose, whatever it might be. We were not left long in doubt. Hoisting the sails, and cutting the cable of the anchor, they sailed our vessel to an island which lay a little further off, and they drove us ashore.

Then they made off in the ship, leaving us helpless upon the shore. It was a place all seamen regarded with horror – for a reason which you will soon learn.

Turning away from the sea we wandered miserably inland, finding as we went various herbs and fruits which we ate, feeling that we might as well live as long as possible, even though we had no hope of escape. Presently we saw in the far distance what seemed to be a splendid palace, towards which we turned our weary steps. But when we reached it we saw that it was a castle, very tall and strongly built. Pushing back the heavy ebony doors, we entered the courtyard. But upon the threshold of the great hall beyond it we paused, frozen with horror, at the sight which greeted us.

On one side lay a huge pile of bones – human bones – and on the other numberless spits for roasting! Overcome with despair we sank trembling to the ground, and lay there too frightened to move. The sun was setting when a loud noise aroused us. The door of the hall burst violently open and a horrible giant entered. He was as tall as a palm tree, perfectly black, and had one eye, which flamed like a burning coal in the middle of his forehead. His teeth were long and sharp

and grinned horribly, while his lower lip hung down upon his chest. He had ears like an elephant's which covered his shoulders, and nails like the claws of some fierce bird.

At this terrible sight our senses left us and we lay like dead men.

Whearingen at last we came to ourselves, the giant sat examining us attentively with his fearful eye. Presently he came towards us and, stretching out his hand, took me by the back of the neck, turning me this way and that. Feeling that I was mere skin and bone he set me down again and went on to one of my companions, whom he treated in the same fashion. At last he came to the captain, and found him to be the fattest of us all. So he took him up in one hand, stuck him upon a spit and roasted him over a huge fire before devouring him hungrily. After the giant had eaten he lay down to sleep, snoring like the loudest thunder, while we lay shivering with horror the whole night through. When day broke he awoke and went out, leaving us in the castle.

When he was gone we started bemoaning our horrible fate, until the hall echoed with our despairing cries. Although there were many of us and he was alone, it did not occur to us to kill him, for there seemed no way we could do it. So at last, submitting to our sad fate, we spent the day in wandering up and down the island eating what fruits we could find. And when night came we returned to the castle, for we knew there was nowhere we could hide to escape the giant.

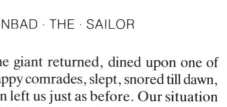

At sunset the giant returned, dined upon one of our unhappy comrades, slept, snored till dawn, and then left us just as before. Our situation seemed so frightful that several of my companions thought it would be better to leap from the cliffs and perish in the waves at once, rather than await so miserable an end. But I had a plan of escape which I explained to them – it seemed our only chance of attacking the giant successfully.

'Listen, my brothers,' I added once I had told them of my plan. 'Let us make several rafts of the driftwood that lies along the shore, and carry them to a suitable place. If our plot succeeds, we can wait patiently for some passing ship to rescue us from this fatal island. If it fails, we must quickly take to our rafts. Frail as they are, we have more chance of saving our lives that way than by staying here.'

All agreed with me, and we spent the day building rafts, each capable of carrying three people. At nightfall we returned to the castle, and very soon in came the giant, and one more of us was taken. But the time of our revenge was at hand! As soon as he had finished his horrible meal he lay down to sleep. When we heard him begin to snore I, and nine of my boldest comrades, rose softly. We each took a spit, which we made red-hot in the fire, and then plunged them with one accord into the giant's eye, completely blinding him.

With a terrible cry, he sprang to his feet clutching in all directions to try to seize one of us. But we had all fled different ways, and thrown ourselves flat upon the ground in corners where he could not touch us with his feet.

After a vain search he fumbled about till he found the door, and fled out of it howling at the top of his voice. As for us, when he was gone we quickly left the fatal castle and, stationing ourselves beside our rafts, waited to see what would happen. Our plan was that if, when the sun rose, we saw nothing of the giant and no longer heard his howls, which still came faintly through the darkness, we should assume that he was dead. Then we could stay safely upon the island and need not risk our lives upon the frail rafts.

But alas! Morning light showed our enemy approaching, supported on either hand by two giants nearly as large and fearful as himself, while a crowd of others followed close upon their heels. Hesitating no longer, we clambered upon our rafts and rowed as fast as we could out to sea. The giants, seeing their prey escaping them, seized huge pieces of rock and waded into the water after us. They hurled the rocks at our rafts with such good aim that all but the one I was upon were swamped, and their luckless crews drowned. There was nothing we could do to help them. It was all the three of us could do to keep our own raft beyond the reach of the giants, but after much hard rowing we at last reached the open sea. Here we were at the mercy of the wind and waves, which tossed us to and fro all that day and night.

The next morning we found ourselves near an island, upon which we gladly landed. There we found delicious fruits and, having satisfied our hunger, lay down to rest upon the shore. Suddenly

we were woken by a loud rustling noise and, starting up, saw that it was an immense snake which was gliding towards us over the sand! So swiftly it came that it had seized one of my comrades before he had time to move and, in spite of his cries and struggles, it speedily crushed the life out of him in its mighty coils and swallowed him whole.

By this time my other companion and I were runing for our lives in search of some place where we would be safe from this new horror. Luckily, we came across a tall tree and climbed up into it, thankful to have escaped certain death. When night came I fell asleep, only to be awakened once more by the terrible snake. After hissing horribly round the tree, it reared itself up against it and, finding my sleeping comrade perched just below me, it swallowed him also and crawled away leaving me half dead with terror.

When the sun rose I crept down from the tree with hardly a hope of escaping the dreadful fate which had overtaken my comrades. But life is sweet, and I determined to do all I could to save myself. All day long I worked as hard as I could, collecting quantities of dry brushwood, reeds and thorns, which I bound in bundles. Then I made a circle of some of them under my tree and piled the rest firmly one upon another until I had a kind of tent in which I crouched like a mouse in a hole until morning came. You may imagine what a fearful night I spent, for the snake returned eager to devour me, and glided round and round my frail shelter seeking an entrance.

Every moment I feared that it would succeed in pushing aside some of the bundles. But happily for me they held together, and when it grew light my enemy retired, baffled and hungry, to his den.

As for me I was more dead than alive! Shaking with fright and half suffocated by the poisonous breath of the monster, I came out of my tent and crawled down to the sea. I felt for a moment that it would be better to plunge from the cliffs and end my life at once rather than pass another night of such horror. But to my joy and relief I saw a ship sailing by and, by shouting wildly and waving my turban, I managed to attract the attention of her crew.

A boat was sent to rescue me, and very soon I found myself on board surrounded by a wondering crowd of sailors and merchants. All were eager to know by what chance I found myself on that desolate island. And after I had told my story, they gave me the choicest food on the ship and the captain, seeing that I was in rags, generously offered me one of his own coats.

After sailing about for some time and touching at many ports, we came at last to the island of Salahat, where sandal wood grows in great abundance. Here we anchored and, as I stood watching the merchants unloading their goods and preparing to sell or exchange them, the captain came up to me and said:

'I have here, brother, some goods belonging to a passenger of mine who is dead. Will you do me the favour of buying them, so when I find his family I shall be able to give them the money. Though, of

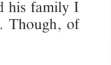

course it will be only fair if you have a portion for your trouble.'

I consented gladly, and he pointed the bales out to me.

'They belonged to a merchant named Sinbad the Sailor,' he added as he turned to go.

At this I was greatly surprised but, looking carefully at him, I realized that – although he was much changed by his travels – he was none other than the captain of the ship upon which I had made my second voyage! As for him, believing me to be dead, it was no wonder that he had not recognised me.

'So, captain,' said I, 'the merchant who owned those bales was called Sinbad?'

'Yes,' he replied. 'That was his name. He came from Bagdad, and joined my ship at Balsora. But by mistake he was left behind upon a desert island where we had landed to fill up our water-casks, and it was not until four hours later that we found he was missing. By that time the wind was blowing strongly, and it was impossible to go back for him.'

'You think he will have perished then?' said I.

'Alas! yes,' he answered.

'Why, captain!' I cried cheerfully, 'look closer and you will see that I am that Sinbad who fell asleep upon the island and woke to find myself abandoned!'

The captain stared at me in amazement. But eventually he was convinced that I was indeed speaking the truth, and rejoiced greatly at my escape.

'I am glad that I need no longer feel guilty about my dreadful carelessness,' he said. 'Now take your goods, and may luck go with you in future.'

I took them gratefully, and we set off on our voyage back home. Once again I saw many wonders along the way. In one place I saw a tortoise which was twenty cubits long and as many broad, in another a fish as big as a cow which had skin so thick that it was used to make shields. And so by degrees we came back to Balsora, and I returned to Bagdad with so much money that I could not count it all, plus treasures without end. I gave again as much as I could to the poor, and bought much land to add to my estate, and so ended my third voyage."

When Sinbad had finished his story he gave another hundred sequins to Hinbad, who departed with the other guests. Then the next day when they had all reassembled and the banquet was ended, their host continued the tale of his adventures.

FOURTH VOYAGE

"Rich and happy as I was after my third voyage, I could not make up my mind to stay at home altogether. My love of trading, and the pleasure I took in anything that was new and strange, made me eager for another journey. So I set off to explore the great Empire of Persia, having first sent off stores of goods to the different places I intended to visit. I boarded a ship at a distant seaport, and for some time all went well, until we were caught in a violent hurricane. The ship was a total wreck in spite

of all our worthy captain did to save her, and many of our company perished in the waves. I, with a few others, had the good fortune to be washed ashore clinging to pieces of the wreck, for the storm had driven us near an island. Scrambling up beyond the reach of the waves we threw ourselves down quite exhausted, to wait for morning.

At daylight we wandered inland, and soon saw some huts, to which we made our way. As we drew near, dozens of black men swarmed out in great numbers and surrounded us. I was taken into one hut with five others and made to sit upon the ground. Then the strangers gave some herbs to us, and made signs for us to eat them. I noticed that they themselves did not touch them, so I was careful only to pretend to taste. But my companions, being very hungry, rashly ate up all that was set before them.

Very soon I had the horror of seeing them become quite mad. Though they chattered on and on, I could not understand a word they said, nor did they take any notice when I spoke to them. The savages now produced large bowls full of rice prepared with coconut oil, which my crazy comrades ate eagerly. But I only tasted a few grains, for I was quite sure that they were just fattening us up for their dinner! My unlucky companions felt neither anxiety nor fear, and ate greedily all that was offered them. Sure enough, in a few days they had grown very fat, and that was the end of them!

I grew leaner day by day, for I ate very little, and was so afraid. And, as I was so far from being a tempting morsel, I was allowed to wander about freely. Then one day, when all my captors had gone off on some expedition, leaving only an old man to guard me, I managed to escape from him. Plunging into the forest, I ran faster the more he cried to me to come back. Soon I had completely escaped him.

For seven days I hurried on, resting only when it was too dark to see, and living chiefly upon coconuts, eating the flesh and drinking their milk. On the eighth day I reached the seashore and saw a party of white men gathering pepper, which grew abundantly all about. I walked towards them and they greeted me in Arabic, asking who I was and where I had come from. I was delighted to hear this familiar speech, and willingly satisfied their curiosity, telling them how I had been shipwrecked and captured.

'But these savages devour men!' they said. 'How did you escape?' So I repeated to them what I have just told you, at which they were astonished. I stayed with them until they had collected as much pepper as they needed, and then they took me back to their own country. There, they presented me to their king who received me kindly. To him I also told my story, which surprised him greatly, and when I had finished he ordered that I should be supplied with food and clothes and treated with consideration.

The island on which I found myself was full of people and abounded in all sorts of desirable things. A great deal of trading went on in the capital, where I soon began to feel at home and

contented. Moreover, the king treated me with special favour so everyone, whether at the court or in the town, sought to make life pleasant for me.

One thing I noticed which I thought very strange was that, from the greatest to the least, all the men rode their horses without bridle or stirrups. One day I presumed to ask his majesty why he did not use them, to which he replied, 'I don't understand you – these are things of which I have never heard!'

This gave me an idea. I found a clever workman, and made him cut out under my direction the foundation of a saddle, which I padded and covered with choice leather, adorning it with rich gold embroidery. I then got a lock-smith to make me a bit and a pair of spurs after a pattern that I drew for him, and when all these things were completed I presented them to the king and showed him how to use them.

When I had saddled one of his horses he mounted it and rode about quite delighted with the idea, and to show his gratitude he rewarded me with large gifts. After this I had to make saddles for all the officers of the king's household and, as they all gave me rich presents, I soon became very wealthy and quite an important person in the city.

O ne day the king sent for me and said, 'Sinbad, I am going to ask a favour of you. Both I and my subjects respect you, and wish you to end your days amongst us. Therefore I desire you to marry a rich and beautiful lady from this wonderful land and to think no more of your own country.'

As the king's will was law, I accepted the charming

bride he presented to me, and lived happily with her. Nevertheless, I had every intention of escaping at the first opportunity, and going back to Bagdad. Things were thus going well with me when it happened that the wife of one of my neighbours, with whom I had struck up quite a friendship, fell ill and presently died. I went to his house to offer my consolations, and found him in the depths of woe.

'Heaven preserve you,' said I, 'and send you a long life!'

'Alas!' he replied, 'what is the good of saying that when I have but an hour left to live?'

'Come, come!' said I, 'surely it is not so bad as all that. I trust that you may live to be my friend for many years.'

'I hope,' he answered, 'that *your* life may be long, but as for me, all is finished. I have set my house in order, and to-day I shall be buried with my wife. This has been the law upon our island from the earliest ages – the living husband goes to the grave with his dead wife, the living wife with her dead husband. This is what our fathers did, and so must we. The law will not change, and all must submit to it!'

As he spoke, the friends and relations of the un-happy pair began to assemble. The body of his wife, decked in rich robes and sparkling with jewels, was laid upon an open bier, and the procession started. It headed for a high mountain some distance from the city, and the wretched husband, clothed from head to foot in a black mantle, followed sorrowfully behind.

When the burial place was reached the corpse was lowered, just as it was, into a deep pit. Then the husband, bidding farewell to all his friends, stretched himself upon another bier, upon which were laid seven little loaves of bread and a pitcher of water. Then he also was let down-down-down into the depths of the horrible cavern and a great stone was laid over the opening. This done, the sad crowd made its way back to the city.

You may imagine how I felt watching this – to the others it was something they had been used to from their youth up – but I was so horrified that I could not help telling the king how it struck me.

'Sire,' I said, 'I am more astonished than I can express to you at the strange custom which exists in your land of burying the living with the dead. In all my travels I have never before met with so cruel and horrible a law.'

'What would you have, Sinbad?' he replied. 'It is the law for everybody. I myself should be buried with the Queen if she were the first to die.'

'But, your Majesty,' said I, 'dare I ask if this law applies to foreigners also?'

'Why, yes,' replied the king smiling, in what I felt was a very heartless manner, 'they are no exception to the rule if they have married in the country.'

When I heard this I went home feeling very unhappy, and from that time forward was greatly troubled. If only my wife's little finger ached I fancied she was going to die, and sure enough before very long she fell really ill and in a few days had died of a great fever. My dismay was great, for it seemed to me that being buried alive was a far worse fate than being eaten by cannibals – but there was no escape.

The body of my wife, arrayed in her richest robes and decked with all her jewels, was laid upon a bier. I followed it, and after me came a great procession, headed by the king and all his nobles. And in this order we reached the fatal mountain, which was one of a tall chain bordering the sea.

Here I made one more frantic effort to appeal to the pity of the king and those who stood by, hoping to save myself even at this last moment. But it was no use. No one spoke to me, they even appeared to move more quickly over their dreadful task, and I speedily found myself descending into the gloomy pit with my seven loaves and pitcher of water beside me.

Almost before I reached the bottom, the stone was rolled into its place above my head, and I was left to my fate. A feeble ray of light shone into the cavern through some chink, and when I had the courage to look about me I could see that I was in a vast vault. All around me lay the bones and bodies of other poor souls and I even fancied that I could hear the dying sighs of those who, like myself, had come into this dismal place alive. All in vain I shrieked aloud with rage and despair, reproaching myself for the love of

gain and adventure which had brought me to such a place. But at length, growing calmer, I took up my bread and water and, wrapping my face in my mantle, I groped my way towards the end of the cavern, where the air was fresher.

Here I lived in darkness and misery until my provisions were exhausted. But just as I was about to die from starvation the rock was rolled away overhead and I saw that a bier was being lowered into the cavern. The corpse upon it was a man and in a moment my mind was made up. The woman who followed had nothing to expect but a lingering death, so I should be doing her a service if I shortened her misery. When she descended, already senseless with terror, I was ready armed with a huge bone, one blow from which left her dead. I took her bread and water, which gave me some hope of life.

I do not know how long I had been a prisoner when one day I fancied that I heard something near me, breathing loudly. Turning to the place from which the sound came I dimly saw a shadowy form which fled at my movement, squeezing itself through a cranny in the wall. I pursued it as fast as I could, and found myself in a narrow crack among the rocks, along which I was just able to force my way.

I followed it for what seemed to me many miles, and at last saw before me a glimmer of light which grew clearer every moment. At last I emerged upon a sea shore with a joy I cannot describe. When I was sure that I was not dreaming, I realised that my guide must have been some little animal which had found

its way into the cavern from the sea. When I disturbed it, it had fled, showing me a means of escape which I would never have discovered for myself. I thanked the Lord for his blessing and hastily looked around to make sure that I was safe from being seen from the town.

T he mountains sloped sheer down to the sea, and there was no road across them. So, certain of my safety, I returned to the cavern, and discovered a rich treasure of diamonds, rubies, emeralds, and jewels of all kinds which covered the ground. These I made up into bales, and stored them in a safe place upon the beach. Then I settled down to wait hopefully for the passing of a ship. Two days passed and still there was no sign of rescue. Then, at last, with great delight I saw a vessel not very far from the shore. By waving my arms and shouting loudly, I attracted the attention of her crew.

A boat was sent off to me, and in answer to the questions of the sailors as to how I came to be in such a plight, I replied that I had been shipwrecked two days earlier, but had managed to scramble ashore with the bales which I pointed out to them. Luckily for me they believed my story and, without even looking at the place where they found me, took up my bundles, and rowed me back to the ship. Once on board, I soon saw that the captain was much too busy coping with the ship to pay much attention to me, though he generously made me welcome, and would not even accept the jewels with which I offered to pay my passage.

Our voyage was prosperous and, after visiting many

lands and collecting in each place great stores of goods, I found myself at last in Bagdad, once more with unheard of riches of every description. Again I gave large sums of money to the poor, and gifts to all the mosques in the city, after which I spent my time with my friends and relations, feasting and being richly entertained."

Here Sinbad paused, and his audience declared that the adventures of his fourth voyage had interested them even more than anything they had heard before. They then took their leave, followed by Hinbad, who had once more received a hundred sequins. With the rest, he was asked to return next day for the story of the fifth voyage and gladly agreed.

When the time came, all were in their places. And when they had eaten and drunk all that was set before them, Sinbad continued with his tale.

FIFTH VOYAGE

Not even all that I had gone through could make me contented with a quiet life. I was soon tired of its pleasures, and longed for change and adventure. Therefore I set out once more, but this time in a ship of my own, which I built and fitted out at the nearest seaport. I wished to be able to call at whatever port I chose, taking my own time. But as I did not intend to carry enough goods for a full cargo, I invited several merchants of different nations to join me.

We set sail with the first favourable wind and, after a long voyage upon the open seas, we landed upon an unknown island. There were no people there, so we decided to explore, and had not gone far when we found a roc's egg, as large as the one I had seen before. It was obviously about to hatch, for the beak of the young bird had already pierced the shell. In spite of all I could say to stop them, the merchants who were with me fell upon it with their hatchets, breaking the shell, and killing the young roc. Then, lighting a fire upon the ground, they hacked morsels from the bird, and proceeded to roast them. I stood by in horror, for I knew this would bring terrible bad luck.

Scarcely had they finished their ill-fated meal, when the air above us was darkened by two mighty shadows. The captain of my ship, knowing by experience what this meant, cried out to us that the parent birds were coming, and urged us to get on board with all speed. This we did, and the sails were hoisted. But before we had made any distance the rocs reached their robbed nest and hovered above it, uttering frightful cries when they discovered what had happened to their offspring.

For a moment we lost sight of them, and were flattering ourselves that we had escaped, when suddenly they reappeared and soared into the air directly over our ship. We saw that each held in its claws an immense rock ready to crush us! There was a moment of breathless suspense, then one bird loosed its hold and the huge block of stone hurtled through the air. Thanks to the skill and speed of the helmsman, who

turned our ship violently in another direction, it fell into the sea close beside us, breaking a path through the water till we could nearly see the bottom.

We had hardly time to draw a breath of relief before the other rock fell with a mighty crash right in the middle of our luckless ship, smashing it into a thousand fragments, and hurling both passengers and crew into the sea. I myself went down with the rest, but had the good fortune to rise unhurt. By holding on to a piece of driftwood with one hand and swimming with the other, I kept myself afloat and was soon washed up by the tide on to an island. Its shores were steep and rocky, but I scrambled up safely and threw myself down to rest upon the green turf.

When I had recovered I began to look around the spot in which I found myself, and truly it seemed that I had reached a garden of delights. There were trees everywhere, all laden with colourful flowers and fruit, and a crystal stream wandered in and out under their shadow. When night came I slept sweetly in a cosy nook, though the thought that I was alone in a strange land made me sometimes

start up and look around me in alarm. Then I wished
heartily that I had stayed at home.

However, the morning sunlight restored my courage
and I once more wandered among the trees, always
anxious about what I might see next. I had walked
some distance inland when I saw an old man sitting
upon the river bank. He was obviously frail and at
first I took him to be some ship-wrecked sailor like
myself. I greeted him in a friendly way, but he only
nodded his head at me in reply. I then asked what he
did on the island, but he simply made signs to me that
he wished to get across the river to gather some fruit,
and begged me to carry him on my back.

Pitying his feebleness, I took him up and waded
across the stream. Then I bent down so that he might
more easily reach the bank, and told him to get down.
But instead of letting me set him on his feet (even
now it makes me laugh to think of it!), this creature
who had seemed to me so weak, leaped nimbly onto
my shoulders and hooked his legs round my neck.

He gripped me so tightly that I was nearly choked
and so overcome with terror that I fell senseless to the
ground. When I recovered, my enemy was still there,
though he had released his hold enough to allow me
breathing space. Seeing me revive he prodded me first
with one foot and then with the other, until I was forced
to get up and stagger about, carrying him under the
trees while he gathered and ate the choicest fruits.

This went on all day, and even at night – for when I
threw myself down half dead with weariness, the
terrible old man held on tight to my neck. At the first
glimmer of morning light he drummed me with his

49

heels until I awoke, and was forced to resume my dreary march, day after day.

I t happened one day that I passed a tree under which lay several dry gourds and, picking one up, I amused myself with scooping out its contents to make a hollow cup. Into this I pressed the juice of several bunches of grapes and when it was full, I left it propped in the fork of a tree. A few days later, carrying the hateful old man as usual, I snatched at my gourd as I passed it. It had turned into excellent wine, so good and refreshing that once I drank it I even forgot what I was carrying, and began to sing and dance.

T he old monster was not slow to see the effect which my drink had produced and noticed that I carried him more lightly than usual. He stretched out his skinny hand and, seizing the gourd, first tasted its contents cautiously, then drained them to the very last drop. The wine was so strong that he also began to sing, and soon I felt the iron grip of his goblin legs unclasp. With one vigorous effort I threw him to the ground, and he never moved again!

I was so happy to have at last got rid of this queer old man that I ran leaping and bounding down to the sea shore where, by the greatest good luck, I met with some sailors who had anchored off the island to enjoy the delicious fruits, and to renew their supply of water.

They heard the story of my escape with amazement, saying, 'You fell into the hands of the Old Man of the Sea. It is a mercy indeed that he did not strangle you, as he has everyone else upon whose shoulders he has managed to perch. This island is well known as the scene of his evil deeds, and no merchant or sailor who lands upon it cares to stray far away from the shore.'

After we had talked for a while they took me back with them on board their ship where the captain received me kindly, and we soon set sail.

After several days we reached a large and prosperous-looking town where all the houses were built of stone. Here we anchored and one of the merchants, who had been very friendly to me on the way, took me ashore with him. He then provided me with a large sack, and pointed out to me a group of others who held sacks in their hands.

'Go with them,' said he, 'and do as they do, but beware of losing sight of them, for if you wander your life will be in danger.'

With that he supplied me with food, said farewell, and I set out with my new companions. I soon learnt that the object of our expedition was to fill our sacks with coconuts, but when I saw the trees and noted their immense height and the slippery smoothness of

51

their slender trunks, I did not see how we could do it. The tops of the coco-palms were alive with monkeys, big and little, which skipped from one tree to the other with the greatest ease.

At first I was surprised when my companions began to collect stones and threw them at the lively creatures, which seemed to me quite harmless. But very soon I saw why, for the monkeys began to tear the nuts from the trees and cast them at us in anger. This meant, of course, that with very little effort our sacks were soon filled with the fruit we wanted.

As soon as we had as much as we could carry, we went back to the town where some merchants bought my share. And so I continued to do this work until I had earned money enough to take me home. Just then I heard that there was a trading ship ready to sail and, taking leave of my friend I went on board, carrying with me a good store of coconuts.

We sailed first to the islands where pepper grows, then to Comari where the best aloes wood is found. And so I exchanged my nuts for pepper and good aloes wood, and went fishing for pearls with some of the other merchants. My divers were so lucky that very soon I had an immense number of these precious jewels from the sea, all of them large and perfect.

So with all these treasures I came joyfully back to Bagdad, where I disposed of them for large sums of money. As before, I gave a tenth part of this to the poor, and after that I rested and comforted myself with all the pleasures that my riches could give me."

Having thus ended his story, Sinbad ordered that one hundred sequins should be given to Hinbad, and the guests then withdrew. But after the next day's feasting, as usual Sinbad began the account of his next adventure.

SIXTH VOYAGE

"It must be a marvel to you how, after I had five times met with shipwreck and unheard of dangers, I could again tempt fortune and risk fresh trouble. I am even surprised myself when I look back, but after a year of rest I prepared to make a sixth voyage – despite the wishes of my friends and relations, who did all they could to keep me at home.

Instead of going by the Persian Gulf, I travelled overland, and set sail from a distant Indian port with a captain who meant to make a long voyage. And truly he did so, for we fell in with stormy weather which drove us completely off course, so for many days neither captain nor pilot knew where we were, nor where we were going. When they at last discovered our position we had no reason to rejoice. The captain, casting his turban upon the deck and tearing at his beard, declared that we were in the most dangerous spot upon the whole wide sea, and had been caught by a current which was sweeping us to destruction. It was too true!

In spite of all the sailors could do we were driven with frightful speed towards the foot of a mountain which rose sheer out of the sea, and our

vessel was dashed to pieces upon the rocks at its base. However, we managed to scramble to the shore, carrying with us the most precious of our possessions. But, as we lay breathless among the rocks, the captain said to us:

'Now we are here we may as well begin to dig our graves at once, since from this fatal spot no ship-wrecked mariner has ever returned!'

This speech discouraged us so much that we began to cry miserably at our sad fate.

The mountain lay on the seaward side of a large island, and the narrow strip of rocky shore upon which we stood was strewn with the wreckage of a thousand gallant ships. The bones of luckless mariners shone white in the sunshine, and we shuddered to think how soon our own would be added to the heap. All around, too, lay vast quantities of costly goods, and treasures were heaped in every cranny of the rocks, yet all these useless riches seemed only to make the scene more desolate.

It struck me as very strange that a river of clear fresh water, which gushed out from the mountain not far from where we stood, did not flow into the sea as rivers generally do, but turned off sharply and flowed out of sight under a natural archway of rock. When I went to examine it more closely, I found that the walls inside the cave were thick with diamonds, and rubies, and masses of crystal, and the floor was strewn with ambergris. Here, then, upon this desolate shore we abandoned ourselves to our fate. There was no possibility of climbing the mountain, and even if a ship

appeared it would only be destroyed as ours had been. The first thing our captain did was to divide equally amongst us all the food we possessed, so the length of each man's life depended on the time he could make his portion last.

s the days passed, one by one my companions died. And by the time I had buried the last one, my own stock of provisions was so small that I hardly expected to live long enough to dig my own grave. I set about doing just this, while regretting bitterly the urge to wander that always brought me into such dire situations.

Then, luckily for me, the fancy took me to stand once more beside the river where it plunged out of sight into the depths of the cavern, and as I did so an idea struck me. This river which hid itself underground must emerge again at some distant spot. So why should I not build a raft and trust myself to its swiftly flowing waters? If I perished before I could reach the light of day once more I should be no worse off than I was now, for death stared me in the face. And there was always the possibility that, as I was born under a lucky star, I might find myself safe and sound.

I decided at any rate to risk it, and speedily built myself a stout raft of driftwood bound with strong cords, from the wreckage which lay strewn upon the beach. I then made up many packages of rubies, emeralds, rock crystal, ambergris, and other precious things, and bound them upon my raft. Finally, with fear in my heart, I seated myself upon it, held tightly to two small oars that I had made, and loosened the

cord which held the raft to the bank. Once out in the current it flew swiftly under the gloomy archway, and I found myself in total darkness, carried smoothly forward by the rapid river.

On I went, for what seemed many nights and many days. Once the channel became so small that I narrowly escaped being crushed against the rocky roof, and after that I took the precaution of lying flat upon my precious bales. Though I only ate what was absolutely necessary to keep myself alive, the inevitable moment came when, after swallowing my last morsel of food, I began to wonder if I would die of hunger after all. Then, worn out with anxiety and fatigue, I fell into a deep sleep.

When I again opened my eyes I was once more in the light of day. A beautiful country lay before me and my raft, which was tied to the river bank, was surrounded by friendly looking black men. I rose and saluted them and they spoke to me in return, but I could not understand a word of their language. Feeling perfectly bewildered by my sudden return to life and light, I murmured to myself in Arabic, 'Close thine eyes, and while thou sleepest Heaven will change thy fortune from evil to good.'

O)ne of the natives, who understood this language, then came forward saying:

'My brother, do not be surprised to see us. This is our land, and as we came to get water from the river we noticed your raft floating down it, and one of us swam out and brought you to the shore. We have waited for you to wake. Tell us now where you come from and where you were going to in such a dangerous fashion?'

I replied that nothing would please me better than to tell them, but that I was starving and had not eaten properly for days. I was soon supplied with all I needed and, having satisfied my hunger, I told them faithfully all that had happened. They were lost in wonder when my tale was translated to them, and said that I must tell their king of my adventures. So they mounted me on a horse, and we set out, followed by several strong men who carried my raft upon their shoulders.

I)n this way we marched into the city of Serendib, where the natives presented me to their king. I saluted him in the Indian fashion, laying myself at his feet and kissing the ground, but the monarch bade me rise and sit beside him, asking first what was my name.

'I am Sinbad,' I replied. 'Men call me "the Sailor", for I have voyaged much upon many seas.'

'And how do you come here?' asked the king.

I told my story, concealing nothing, and his surprise and delight were so great that he ordered my adventures to be written in letters of gold and placed in the great library of his kingdom.

Presently my raft was brought in and the bales opened in his presence. The king declared that in all his treasury there were no such rubies and emeralds as those which lay in great heaps before him. Seeing that he looked at them with interest, I said that I myself and all that I had were at his disposal, but he answered me smiling:

'No, Sinbad. Heaven forbid that I should desire to take your riches. I would rather add to them, for you shall not leave my kingdom without some tokens of my good will.' He then commanded his officers to provide me with suitable lodgings at his expense, and sent slaves to wait upon me and carry my raft and treasures to my new dwelling place.

You may imagine that I was truly grateful, and visited the king every day to amuse him with my stories. For the rest of my time I amused myself in seeing the sights of the city.

The island of Serendib is sited on the line of the equinox, which means that the days and nights there are of equal length. The chief city is placed at the end of a beautiful valley, formed by the highest mountain in the world which is in the middle of the island. I was curious to climb to the very top, for I had been told that this was where Adam was sent when he was banished from Paradise. Here I found rubies and many precious things, and rare plants growing abundantly, with cedar trees and cocoa palms. On the seashore and at the mouths of the rivers, divers seek for pearls, and in some valleys the rocks are studded with diamonds.

But despite such beauty, after many days I asked the king if I could return to my own country, to which he consented. He loaded me with rich gifts, and when I went to take leave of him he entrusted me with a royal present and a letter to the ruler of my own fair land, saying, 'Please give these to the Caliph Haroun al Raschid, and assure him of my friendship.'

I accepted this duty, and soon set sail upon the ship which the king himself had chosen. The king's letter was written in blue upon a rare and precious skin of yellowish colour, and this is what it said:

'The King of the Indies, before whom walk a thousand elephants, who lives in a palace where the roof blazes with a hundred thousand rubies, and whose treasure house contains twenty thousand diamond crowns, to the Caliph Haroun al Raschid sends greeting. Though the offering we present to you is unworthy of your notice, we pray you to accept it as a mark of the respect and friendship which we hold for you.'

The present consisted of a vase carved from a single ruby, six inches high and almost as many wide. This was filled with the choicest pearls – large, and of perfect shape and lustre. Next there came a huge snake skin, with scales as large as a sequin, which would preserve from sickness anyone who slept upon it. There were also quantities of aloes wood, camphor, and pistachio-nuts and, lastly, a beautiful slave girl, whose robes glittered with precious stones.

After a long and prosperous voyage we landed at Balsora, and I made haste to reach Bagdad. Taking the king's letter I presented myself at the palace gate, followed by the beautiful slave, and various members of my own family bearing the treasure.

As soon as I had declared my errand I was taken into the presence of the Caliph, to whom I bowed low and gave the letter and the king's gift. When he had examined them, he demanded of me whether the Prince of Serendib was really as rich and powerful as he claimed to be.

'Commander of the Faithful,' I replied, again bowing humbly before him, 'I can assure your Majesty that he has in no way exaggerated his wealth and grandeur. Nothing can equal the magnificence of his palace. When he goes abroad his throne is prepared upon the back of an elephant, and on either side of him ride his minister, his favourites, and courtiers. On his elephant's neck sits an officer, his golden lance in his hand, and behind him stands another bearing a pillar of gold, at the top of which is an emerald as long as my hand. A thousand men in cloth of gold, mounted upon richly dressed elephants, go before him. He is the Sultan of the Indies, and all his people love him as a just ruler.'

The Caliph was well satisfied with my report.

'From the king's letter,' said he, 'I judged that he was a wise man. It seems that he is worthy of his

people, and his people of him.'

So saying he dismissed me with rich presents, and I returned in peace to my own house."

When Sinbad had finished speaking his guests withdrew, Hinbad having first received a hundred sequins. But all returned next day to hear the story of the seventh voyage.

 SEVENTH & LAST VOYAGE

"After my sixth voyage I was quite determined that I would go to sea no more. I was now of an age to appreciate a quiet life, and had run risks enough. I only wished to end my days in peace. One day, however, when I was entertaining a number of my friends, I was told that an officer of the Caliph wished to speak to me. He asked me to follow him into the presence of Haroun al Raschid, the Caliph himself and of course I obeyed. After I had saluted him, the Caliph said:

'I have sent for you, Sinbad, because I need your services. I have chosen you to bear a letter and gift to the King of Serendib in return for his message of friendship.' The Caliph's commandment fell upon me like a thunderbolt.

'Commander of the Faithful,' I answered, 'I am ready to do all that your Majesty asks, but I humbly pray you to remember all the unheard of sufferings I have undergone. Indeed, I have made a vow never again to leave Bagdad.'

With this I gave him a long account of some of my adventures, to which he listened patiently.

'I admit,' said he, 'that you have indeed had some strange times on your travels, but I do not see why they should stop you from doing as I wish. You have only to go straight to Serendib and deliver my message, then you are free to come back and do as you will. But go you must; my honour demands it.'

Seeing that there was nothing I could do, I accepted his orders and the Caliph, delighted at having got his own way, gave me a thousand sequins for the expenses of the voyage. I was soon ready to start and, taking the letter and the present, I embarked at Balsora and sailed quickly and safely to Serendib. Here, I was well received, and taken immediately to see the king, who greeted me with great joy.

'Welcome, Sinbad,' he cried. 'I have thought of you often, and rejoice to see you once more.'

After thanking him for the honour that he did me, I displayed the Caliph's gifts. First, a bed complete with golden hangings which cost a thousand sequins, and another like it in crimson fabric. Next, fifty robes of rich embroidery, and a hundred of the finest white linen from Cairo, Suez, Cufa and Alexandria. Then more beds of different fashion, and an agate vase carved with the figure of a man aiming an arrow at a lion. And finally a costly table, which had once belonged to King Solomon himself.

The King of Serendib was very satisfied with these gifts and now my task was finished, I was anxious

to depart, but it was some time before the king would think of letting me go. At last, however, he dismissed me with many presents, and I lost no time in going on board a ship. We set sail for Bagdad at once, and for four days all went well.

But on the fifth day we found ourselves at the mercy of some devilish pirates, who seized our vessel. They made prisoners of those who were sensible enough to submit – of whom I was one. When they had taken all we possessed, they forced us to put on horrible rags and sailed to a distant island where they sold us for slaves. I luckily fell into the hands of a rich merchant, who took me home with him, and clothed and fed me well. After some days he sent for me and asked what I could do.

I answered that I was a rich merchant who had been captured by pirates, and therefore I knew no trade.

'Tell me,' he said, 'can you shoot with a bow?'

I replied that I had done so in my youth, and that with practice my skill would probably come back to me.

Upon this he gave me a bow and arrows and, mounting me with him upon his own elephant, took the path to a vast forest which lay far from the town. When we had reached the wildest part of it we stopped, and my master said to me:

'This forest swarms with elephants. Hide yourself in this great tree, and shoot at all that pass you. When you have succeeded in killing one, come and tell me.'

So saying, he gave me a supply of food and returned to the town, while I perched myself high up in the tree and kept watch. That night I saw nothing, but just after sunrise the next morning a large herd of elephants came crashing and trampling by. I lost no time in letting fly several arrows, and at last one of the great animals fell to the ground dead.

The others retreated, leaving me free to come down from my hiding place and run back to tell my master of my success. For this I was praised and given all kinds of good things. Then we went back to the forest together and dug a mighty trench in which we buried the elephant I had killed, so that when it became a skeleton my master might return and take its tusks.

For two months I hunted thus, and no day passed without my killing an elephant. Of course I did not always put myself in the same tree, but sometimes in one place, sometimes in another. One morning as I watched the coming of the elephants I was surprised to see that, instead of passing the tree I was in as they usually did, they paused. Soon they had completely surrounded it, trumpeting horribly, and shaking the very ground with their heavy tread. When I saw that their eyes were fixed upon me I was terrified, and my arrows dropped from my trembling hand. I had good reason to be frightened for, an instant later, the largest of the animals wound his

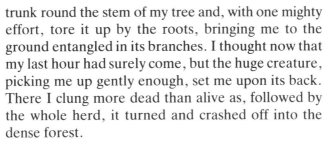

trunk round the stem of my tree and, with one mighty
effort, tore it up by the roots, bringing me to the
ground entangled in its branches. I thought now that
my last hour had surely come, but the huge creature,
picking me up gently enough, set me upon its back.
There I clung more dead than alive as, followed by
the whole herd, it turned and crashed off into the
dense forest.

It seemed to me a long time before I was set upon
my feet again, and I stood as if in a dream while
the herd turned and trampled off in another direction, soon to be hidden amongst the dense trees.
Then, recovering myself, I looked about me and
found that I was standing upon the side of a great
hill, strewn as far as I could see on either hand with
the bones and tusks of elephants.

'This then must be the elephants' burying place,' I
said to myself, 'and they must have brought me here
in the hope that I might cease to persecute them. I
want nothing but their tusks, and here lie more than I
could carry away in a lifetime.'

Whereupon I turned and made for the city as fast
as I could go. I did not see a single elephant along the
way, which convinced me further that they had retired
deeper into the forest to leave the way open to the
Ivory Hill. I was full of admiration for how wise they
were. After a day and a night I reached my master's
house, and was met with joyful surprise.

'Ah! poor Sinbad,' he cried, 'I was wondering
what could have become of you. When I went to the
forest I found the tree newly uprooted, and the arrows

lying beside it. I feared I should never see you again. Pray tell me how you escaped death.'

I soon explained, and the next day we went together to the Ivory Hill, and he was overjoyed to find that I had told him the truth. When we had loaded our elephant with as many tusks as it could carry and were on our way back to the city, he said:

'My brother – I can no longer treat as a slave someone who has brought me so many riches. Take your freedom and may Heaven bless you. These wild elephants have killed many of our slaves every year. No matter what good advice we gave them, they were caught sooner or later. You alone have escaped these animals, and therefore must be under the special protection of Heaven. Now through you the whole town will be wealthy without further loss of life.'

Overcome with joy I replied, 'Master, I thank you, and wish you all prosperity. For myself I only ask for freedom to return to my own country.'

'So it shall be,' he answered. 'The monsoon winds will soon bring the ivory ships to our island, and then I will send you on your way.'

So I stayed with him till the time of the monsoon, and every day we added to our store of ivory till all his warehouses were overflowing. By this time the other merchants knew the secret, but there was enough treasure for all. When the ships at last arrived my master himself chose the one in which I was to sail, and put on board for me a great store of wonderful food, a large quantity of ivory and many costly treasures. And so we parted.

I left the ship at the first port we came to, not feeling at ease upon the sea after all that had happened to me on my sailing voyages. Having sold my ivory for much gold, and bought many rare and expensive presents, I loaded my pack animals and joined a caravan of merchants. Our journey was long and dull, but I bore it patiently, reflecting that at least I had nothing to fear from tempests, nor pirates, nor serpents, nor any of the other perils from which I had suffered before. And at length we reached Bagdad.

My first concern was to present myself before the Caliph, and to give him an account of my visit. He assured me he had been worried about my long absence, but had nevertheless hoped for the best. As to my adventure among the elephants, he heard it with amazement!

By his orders this story and all the others I had told him were written up in letters of gold, and laid among his treasures. I took my leave of him, well satisfied with the honours and rewards he had given me, and since that time have given myself up to my family and my friends."

Thus Sinbad ended the story of his seventh and last voyage, and turning to Hinbad he added:

'Well, my friend, what do you think now? Have you ever heard of anyone who has suffered more, or had more narrow escapes than I have? Is it not just that I should now enjoy a life of ease and peace?'

Hinbad drew near and, kissing his hand respect-fully, replied, 'Sir, you have indeed known fearful perils. My troubles have been nothing compared to yours. Moreover, the generous use you make of your wealth by giving so much to the poor, proves that you deserve it. May you live long and happily.'

Sinbad then gave him a hundred sequins, and hence-forth counted him among his friends. As for Hinbad, he was wealthy enough now, thanks to the kindness of the great man, to give up his profession as a porter. He spent the rest of his days living in peace and comfort and never did he forget the great adventures of his friend Sinbad the Sailor.

ALADDIN
& THE
MAGIC LAMP

There once lived a poor tailor, who had a son called Aladdin, a careless, idle boy who would do nothing but play all day long in the streets with little idle boys like himself. This made the father so unhappy that he died of grief. But in spite of his mother's tears and prayers, Aladdin did not mend his ways.

One day, when he was playing in the streets as usual, a stranger asked him his age, and if he were not the son of Mustapha the tailor.

'I am, sir,' replied Aladdin, 'but he died a long while ago.'

At this the stranger hugged and kissed him, saying, 'I am your uncle, and knew you from your likeness to my brother. Go to your mother and tell her I am coming.'

Aladdin ran home, and told his mother of his newly-found uncle.

'Indeed, child,' she said, 'your father had a brother, but I always thought he was dead.' How could she have known that this was no uncle, but instead a cunning African magician?

She hurried to prepare their supper, and Aladdin ran off eagerly to fetch their guest, who came laden with wine and fruit.

'Do not be surprised that we have never met before,' he said to Aladdin's trusting mother, 'for I have been on my travels for forty years.'

He then turned to Aladdin and asked him his trade, at which the boy hung his head, while his mother

burst into tears. On learning that Aladdin was idle and would learn no trade, he offered to buy a shop for him and stock it with goods.

Next day he bought Aladdin a fine suit of clothes, and took him all over the city, showing him the sights. He brought him home at nightfall to his mother, who was overjoyed to see her son looking so fine.

Next day the magician led Aladdin into some beautiful gardens a long way outside the city gates. They sat down by a fountain, and the magician pulled a cake from his girdle, which he divided between them. Then they journeyed onwards till they almost reached the mountains. Aladdin was so tired that he begged to go back, but the magician kept him amused with pleasant stories, and led him on for many more miles.

At last they came to two mountains divided by a narrow valley.

'We will go no farther,' said the false uncle. 'Now I will show you something wonderful. Please gather up some sticks while I kindle a fire.'

When it was lit the magician drew a powder from his pocket and threw it on the flames, saying some strange magical words. The earth trembled a little and opened in front of them, disclosing a square flat stone with a brass ring in the middle to raise it by. Aladdin was dreadfully afraid and tried to run away, but the magician caught him and gave him a blow that knocked him to the ground.

'What have I done, uncle?' he said piteously, where-upon the magician said more kindly, 'Fear nothing, but obey me. Beneath this stone lies a treasure which is to be yours, and no one else may touch it, so you must do exactly as I tell you.'

At the word treasure, Aladdin forgot his fears, and grasped the ring as he was told, saying the names of his father and grandfather. The stone came up quite easily and some steps appeared, leading down into a dark cave.

'Go down,' said the magician. 'At the foot of these steps you will find an open door leading into three large halls. Tuck up your gown and go through them without touching anything, or you will die instantly. These halls lead into a garden of fine fruit trees. Walk on till you come to a niche in a terrace where stands a lighted lamp. Pour out the oil it contains and bring it to me.' With this, he drew a ring from his finger and gave it to Aladdin, saying,

'This is for you. Go safely!'

Aladdin found everything as the magician had said He gathered some fruit off the trees, picked up the lamp and returned to the mouth of the cave. The magician cried out in a great hurry,

'Make haste and give me the lamp!'

But Aladdin was on his guard.

'No – first you must help me out of the cave.'

At this the magician flew into a terrible passion, for his evil plans had been completely ruined. He had

read in his magic books of this wonderful lamp, which would make him the most powerful man in the world. Though he alone knew where to find it, he could only receive it from the hands of another. He had picked out Aladdin for this purpose, taking him for a foolish boy, intending to get the lamp and kill him afterwards. Furious at his failure, he threw some more powder on the fire, muttered more magic words, and the stone rolled back into its place with a dreadful boom! The wicked magician fled far away to Africa, leaving Aladdin trapped in the dark cave.

For two days Aladdin remained in the dark, crying and lamenting. But at last, as he clasped his hands in prayer, he accidentally rubbed the ring which the magician had forgotten to take from him. Immediately an enormous and frightful genie rose out of the earth, saying:

'What wouldst thou with me? I am the Slave of the Ring, and will obey thee in all things.'

Aladdin fearlessly replied, 'Deliver me from this place!' And at once the earth opened, and he found himself outside. As soon as his eyes could bear the light he went home, but he was so exhausted that he fainted on the threshold. When he came to, he told his mother what had passed, and showed her the lamp and the fruits he had gathered in the garden which gleamed and sparkled in the sunlight – for they were really precious stones! Aladdin then asked for some food.

'Alas! child,' his mother said, 'I have no food in the house, but I have spun a little cotton and will go and sell it.'

Aladdin told her to keep her cotton, and said he would sell the lamp instead. But as it was very dirty Aladdin's mother began to clean it, so that it might fetch a higher price. The instant she rubbed the lamp another hideous genie appeared, and asked what he could grant her. She fainted with surprise, but Aladdin, snatching the lamp, said boldly:

'Fetch me something to eat!'

Soon the genie returned with twelve silver plates of rich meats and two silver cups of wine.

'Whence comes this splendid feast?' asked Aladdin's amazed mother when she awoke.

'Ask not, but eat,' replied her son.

So they sat down to breakfast and feasted till it was dinner-time, while Aladdin told his mother about the lamp. She begged him to sell it, and have nothing to do with the genie. 'No,' said Aladdin. 'Since chance has made us aware of its virtues, we will use it and the ring likewise, which I shall always wear on my finger.'

When they had eaten all the genie had brought, Aladdin sold the silver plates one by one, until they had used up all the money they fetched. He then summoned the genie again, who gave him another set of plates, and thus they lived for many years.

One day Aladdin heard a new order had been proclaimed by the Sultan. His daughter the princess wished to leave the palace to bathe in the springs of a beautiful garden nearby, and everyone was to stay at home and close their shutters as she passed to and fro. Aladdin was seized by a desire to see her face, which was very difficult, as she always went veiled. So he hid himself behind the door of the gardens and peeped through a chink. The princess lifted her veil as she went inside, and looked so beautiful that Aladdin fell in love with her at first sight.

He went home so changed that his mother was frightened. He told her he loved the princess so deeply that he could not live without her, and meant to ask her father for her hand in marriage. His mother, on hearing this, burst out laughing, but Aladdin at last persuaded her to go before the Sultan and carry his request. She fetched a napkin and laid in it the magic fruits from the enchanted garden, which sparkled and shone like the most beautiful jewels. She took these with her to please the Sultan and set out on her task. The grand-vizir and the lords of council had just gone in as she entered the hall and placed herself in front of the Sultan. He, however, took no notice of her. She went every day for a week, and stood in the same place.

When the council broke up on the sixth day the Sultan said to his vizir, 'I see a certain woman in the audience-chamber every day carrying something in a napkin. Call her next time, that I may find out what she wants.'

Next day, at a sign from the vizir, she went up to the foot of the throne, and remained kneeling till the Sultan said to her, 'Rise, good woman, and tell me what you want.'

She hesitated, so the Sultan sent away all but the vizir, and bade her speak freely, promising to forgive her beforehand for anything she might say. She then told him of her son's violent love for the princess.

'I prayed him to forget her,' she said, 'but in vain. He threatened to do some desperate deed if I refused to go and ask your Majesty for the hand of the princess. Now I pray you to forgive not me alone, but my son Aladdin.'

The Sultan asked her kindly what she had in the napkin, whereupon she unfolded the jewels and presented them.

He was thunderstruck, and turning to the vizir said, 'What sayest thou? Ought I not to bestow the princess on one who values her at such a price?'

The vizir, who wanted her for his own son, begged the Sultan to wait for three months, hoping that in this time his son would find a way to make a richer present. The Sultan granted this, and told Aladdin's mother that, though he consented to the marriage, she must not appear before him again for three months.

Aladdin waited patiently, but one day, after two months had passed, his mother went into the city to buy oil and found everyone rejoicing. She asked what was going on.

'Do you not know,' was the answer, 'that the son

of the grand-vizir is to marry the Sultan's daughter tonight?'

Breathless, she ran and told Aladdin, who at first was overwhelmed with grief. But presently he thought of the lamp. He rubbed it, and the genie appeared, saying, 'What is thy will?'

Aladdin replied, 'The Sultan has broken his promise to me, and the vizir's son is to have the princess. My command is that tonight you bring here the bride and bridegroom.'

'Master, I obey,' said the genie.

Aladdin then went to his chamber where, sure enough, at midnight the genie transported the bed containing the vizir's son and the princess.

'Take this new-married man,' he said, 'and put him outside in the cold, then return at daybreak.'

Whereupon the genie took the vizir's son out of bed, leaving Aladdin with the princess.

'Fear nothing,' Aladdin said to her. 'You are my wife, promised to me by your unjust father, and no harm shall come to you.'

The princess was too frightened to speak, and passed the most miserable night of her life, while Aladdin lay down beside her and slept soundly. At the appointed hour the genie fetched in the shivering bridegroom, laid him in his place, and transported the bed back to the palace.

Presently the Sultan came to wish his daughter good morning. The unhappy vizir's son jumped up and hid himself, while the princess would not say a word, and was very sorrowful.

The Sultan sent her mother to her, who said, 'Why is it, child, that you will not speak to your father? What has happened?'

The princess sighed deeply, and at last told her mother how, during the night, the bed had been carried into some strange house, and what had passed there. Her mother did not believe her in the least, and told her it was nothing more than a dream.

The following night exactly the same thing happened and next morning, when the princess again refused to speak, the angry Sultan threatened to cut off her head! She then confessed all. The miserable bridegroom also admitted the truth, adding that, dearly as he loved the princess, he would rather die than go through another such fearful night, and wished to be separated from her. His wish was granted, and all the feasting and rejoicing came to an end.

When the three months were over, Aladdin sent his mother to remind the Sultan of his promise. She stood in the same place as before and the Sultan, who had forgotten his promise to Aladdin, at once remembered, and sent for her. On seeing her poverty the Sultan felt less inclined than ever to keep his word, and asked the vizir's advice. He advised him to set so high a value on the princess that no man living could meet it.

The Sultan then turned to Aladdin's mother, saying, 'Good woman, a Sultan must remember his promises, and I will remember mine. But your son must first send me forty basins of gold, brimful of jewels,

carried by forty black slaves, led by as many white ones. And all of them must be splendidly dressed. Tell him that I await his answer.' With that, Aladdin's mother bowed low and went home, thinking all was lost.

She gave Aladdin the message, adding, 'He may wait long enough for your answer!'

'Not so long, mother, as you think,' her son replied. 'I would do a great deal more than that for the princess.' He summoned the genie, and in a few moments the eighty slaves arrived, and filled up the small house and garden.

Aladdin made them set out for the palace, walking two by two, followed by his mother. They were so richly dressed, with such splendid jewels in their girdles, that soon everyone had crowded round to see them and the basins of gold they carried on their heads.

They entered the palace and, after kneeling before the Sultan, stood in a half-circle round the throne with their arms crossed, while Aladdin's mother presented them to the Sultan.

He hesitated no longer, but said, 'Good woman, return and tell your son that I wait for him with open arms.'

She lost no time in telling Aladdin, bidding him

make haste. But Aladdin first called the genie.

'I want a scented bath,' he said, 'a richly embroidered habit, a horse surpassing the Sultan's, and twenty slaves to attend me. Besides this, six slaves, beautifully dressed, to wait on my mother. And, lastly, ten thousand pieces of gold in ten purses.'

No sooner had he said it, than it was done. Aladdin mounted his horse and passed through the streets, ordering the slaves to give away gold as they went. Even those who had played with him in his childhood knew him not, for he had grown so handsome.

 hen the Sultan saw him, he came down from his throne, embraced him, and led him into a hall where a feast was spread, intending to marry him to the princess that very day.

But Aladdin refused, saying, 'I must build a palace fit for her,' and took his leave.

Once home he said to the genie, 'Build me a palace of the finest marble, set with jasper, agate, and other precious stones. In the middle you shall build me a large hall with a dome, its four walls of gold and silver, each side having six windows. Diamonds, rubies and emeralds should be set around each window, all except one, which is to be left unfinished. There must also be stables and horses and grooms and slaves. Go and see about it!'

 laddin's palace was finished the next day, and the genie carried him there and showed him that all his orders had been faithfully carried out. A velvet carpet had even been laid from

Aladdin's palace to the Sultan's. Then Aladdin's mother dressed herself carefully, and walked to the palace with her slaves, while he followed her on horseback. The Sultan sent musicians with trumpets and cymbals to meet them, so that the air resounded with music and cheers. She was taken to the princess, who saluted her and treated her with great honour.

At night the princess said good-bye to her father, and set out on the carpet for Aladdin's palace, with his mother at her side, and followed by the hundred slaves. She was charmed at the sight of Aladdin, who ran to receive her.

'Princess,' he said, 'blame your beauty for my boldness if I have displeased you.'

But the princess was far from angry. She was happy to obey her father and marry the handsome Aladdin. After the wedding had taken place Aladdin led her into the hall, where a splendid feast was spread. They dined together then danced till midnight.

Next day Aladdin invited the Sultan to see the palace. On entering the hall with the four-and-twenty windows, with their rubies, diamonds, and emeralds, he cried:

'It is a world's wonder! There is only one thing that surprises me. Was it by accident that one window was left unfinished?'

'No, sir, by design,' returned Aladdin. 'I wished your Majesty to have the glory of finishing this palace.'

The Sultan was pleased, and sent for the best jewellers in the city. He showed them the unfinished window, and bade them fit it up like the others.

'Sir,' replied their spokesman, 'we cannot find jewels enough.'

The Sultan had his own jewels fetched, which were soon all used, but in a month's time the work was still not half done. Aladdin, knowing that their task was impossible, told them to undo their work and carry the jewels back, and the genie finished the window at his command. The Sultan was surprised to receive his jewels again and visited Aladdin, who showed him the finished window. The Sultan embraced him, but the envious vizir muttered that it was the work of enchantment!

Aladdin soon won the hearts of the people by his gentle bearing. He was made captain of the Sultan's armies, and won several battles for him, but remained modest as before, and lived thus in peace and content-ment for several years.

But far away in Africa the magician was brooding about the magic lamp. By his magic arts, he discovered that Aladdin, instead of perishing miserably in the cave, had escaped, and had married a princess with whom he was living in great honour and wealth. He knew that the poor tailor's son could only have accomplished this by means of the lamp, so he travelled night and day till he reached the capital of China, bent on Aladdin's ruin. As he passed through the town he heard people talking everywhere about a marvellous palace.

'Forgive my ignorance,' he asked them, 'but what is this palace you speak of?'

'Have you not heard of Prince Aladdin's palace,'

was the reply, 'the greatest wonder of the world? I will direct you if you have a mind to see it.'

The magician thanked him and, having seen the palace, knew that it had been raised by the genie of the lamp. At this he became half mad with rage and determined to get hold of the lamp, so again Aladdin would be plunged into the deepest poverty.

Unluckily, Aladdin had gone hunting for eight days, which gave the magician plenty of time. He bought a dozen copper lamps, put them into a basket, and went to the palace crying, 'New lamps for old!' It was such a strange offer that a jeering crowd soon developed and followed him.

The princess, sitting in the hall of the four-and-twenty windows, sent a slave to find out what the noise was about. She came back laughing so much that the princess scolded her.

'Madam,' replied the slave, 'who can help laughing to see an old fool offering to exchange fine new lamps for old ones?'

Another slave, hearing this, said, 'There is an old one on the shelf here which he can have.' And she pointed to the magic lamp, which Aladdin had left behind in the palace. The princess, knowing nothing of its power, laughingly told the slave to take it and make the exchange.

So the slave went and said to the magician: 'Give me a new lamp for this.'

He snatched it and bade the slave take her choice, amid the jeers of the crowd. Little he cared! He hurried out of the city gates to a lonely place, where

he remained till nightfall. Then he pulled out the lamp and rubbed it. The genie appeared, and at the magician's command carried him, together with the palace and the princess in it, to a lonely place in Africa.

Next morning the Sultan looked out of the window towards Aladdin's palace and rubbed his eyes, for it was gone! He sent for the vizir, and asked what had become of it. The vizir looked out too, and was lost in astonishment. This time the Sultan was easily convinced that Aladdin was an enchanter. So he sent thirty men on horseback to fetch Aladdin in chains.

They met him riding home, bound him, and forced him to go with them on foot. But the people who loved Aladdin seized their weapons and followed, determined to see that he came to no harm. He was carried before the Sultan, who ordered the executioner to cut off his head. The executioner made Aladdin kneel down, bandaged his eyes, and raised his huge, curved scimitar to strike.

But at that instant the vizir saw that the crowd had forced their way into the courtyard and were scaling the walls to rescue Aladdin, so he called to the executioner to stay his hand. The people looked so threatening that the Sultan gave way to their demands. He ordered Aladdin to be unbound, and pardoned him in the sight of the crowd.

Aladdin now begged to know what he had done.

'False wretch!' said the Sultan, 'come hither,' and he showed him from the window the place where his palace had stood.

Aladdin was so amazed that he could not say a word.

'Where is my palace and my daughter?' demanded the Sultan. 'For the first I am not so deeply concerned, but my daughter I must have, and you must find her or lose your head.'

Aladdin begged for forty days in which to find her, promising, if he failed, to return and suffer his punishment.

For three days Aladdin wandered about like a madman, asking everyone what had become of his palace, but they only laughed and pitied him. He came to the banks of a river and, feeling quite desperate, decided to throw himself in and end his sorrows. But as he clasped his hands to say his last prayers, he rubbed the magic ring he still wore.

The genie he had seen in the cave appeared, and asked his will.

'Save my life, genie,' said Aladdin, 'and bring my palace back.'

'That is not in my power,' said the genie. 'I am only the slave of the ring – you must ask the slave of the lamp.'

'Even so,' said Aladdin, 'you can still take me to the palace, and set me down under my dear wife's window.' No sooner had he said this than he found himself in Africa, under the window of the princess where he fell asleep out of sheer weariness.

He was awakened by the singing of the birds, and sat thinking of what he should do. He saw plainly that all his misfortunes were due to the loss of the lamp, and vainly wondered who had robbed him of it.

That morning the princess rose early. Once a day she was forced to endure the company of the loathsome magician, but she treated him so harshly that he dared not live in the palace with her. As she was dressing, one of her women looked out and saw Aladdin. The princess ran and flung open the window. She called to Aladdin to come to her, and great was their joy at seeing each other again.

After he had kissed her Aladdin said, 'I beg of you, Princess, in God's name, before we speak of anything else, for your own sake and mine, tell me what has become of the old lamp I left in the hall of four-and-twenty windows?'

'Alas!' she said, 'I am the innocent cause of our sorrows, and told him of the exchange of the lamp and all that followed.

'Now I know,' cried Aladdin, 'that we have to thank the African magician for this! Where is the lamp?'

'He carries it about with him,' said the princess, 'I know, for he pulled it out of his robe to show me. He wishes me to break my faith with you and marry him, saying that you were beheaded by my father's command. He is for ever speaking ill of you, but I only reply by my tears.'

Aladdin comforted her, and left her for a while. He devised a clever plan and, having bought a certain powder, returned to the princess, who let him in by a little side door.

'Put on your most beautiful dress,' he said to her, 'and receive the magician with smiles, leading him to believe that you have forgotten me. Invite him to

dine with you, and say you wish to taste the wine of his country. He will go for some, and while he is gone this is what you must do.'

She listened carefully to Aladdin and, after he had gone, she arrayed herself gaily for the first time since she left China. She put on a girdle and head-dress of diamonds and, seeing in a glass that she looked more beautiful than ever, received the magician. To his great amazement, she said, 'I have made up my mind that Aladdin is dead, and that all my tears will not bring him back to me. I am resolved to mourn no more, and have therefore invited you to dine with me. But I am tired of the wines of China, and would taste those of Africa.'

At this, the magician flew to his cellar as planned and, while he was gone, the princess put the powder Aladdin had given her in her cup. When he returned she asked him to drink her health, handing him her cup in exchange for his as a sign she was reconciled to him.

Before drinking, the magician made her a speech in praise of her beauty, but the princess cut him short, saying:

'Let me drink first, and you shall say what you will afterwards.' She set the cup to her lips and kept it there, while the magician drained his to the dregs and fell back lifeless.

The princess then opened the door to Aladdin, and flung her arms round his neck, but Aladdin gently put her aside, bidding her to leave him, as he had more to do. He then went to the dead magician,

took the lamp out of his robe and commanded the genie to carry the palace and all inside it back to China once again.

The Sultan, who was sitting in his closet, mourning for his lost daughter, looked up and rubbed his eyes, for there stood the palace as before!

Aladdin received him in the hall of the four-and-twenty windows, with the princess at his side. Aladdin told him what had happened, and showed him the dead body of the magician as proof of his story. The Sultan was so delighted at their return that he proclaimed a ten day's feast and it seemed as if Aladdin might now live the rest of his life in peace. But it was not to be.

T he African magician had a younger brother who was, if you can believe it, even more wicked and scheming than himself. He travelled to China to avenge his brother's death, and went to visit a holy woman called Fatima, with a cunning plan in mind. He entered her cell and clapped a dagger to her breast, telling her to rise and do his bidding on pain of death. He then put on her clothes, coloured his face like hers, and put on her veil – then murdered her so she could tell no one of his visit.

He proceeded to the palace of Aladdin and all the people, thinking he was the holy woman, gathered round him, kissing his hands and begging his blessing. When he got to the palace there was such a noise going on that the princess bade her slave look out of the window and ask what was the matter. The slave said it was the holy woman, curing people by her

touch, whereupon the princess, who had long desired
to see Fatima, sent for her.

On seeing the princess, the magician's brother
offered up a prayer for her health and prosperity.
The princess then made him sit by her, and begged
him to stay for a while. The false Fatima, who wished
for nothing better, consented and the princess
offered to show him round the palace. Soon they
came to the jewelled hall and the princess asked him
what he thought of it.

'It is truly beautiful,' said the false Fatima. 'But in
my mind it wants but one thing.'

'And what is that?' said the princess.

'If only an egg from the giant roc,' replied he,
'were hung up from the middle of this dome, it would
be the wonder of the world.

When Aladdin returned from hunting he
found the princess in a very ill humour. He
begged to know what was amiss, and she told
him that all her pleasure in the hall was spoilt for the
want of a roc's egg hanging from the dome.

'If that is all,' replied Aladdin, 'you shall have it.'

He left her and rubbed the lamp and, when the genie
appeared, Aladdin commanded him to fetch a roc's
egg. But instead of granting the wish, the genie gave
such a loud and terrible shriek that the hall shook.

'Wretch!' he cried, 'is it not enough that I have
done everything for you, but you must command me
to steal from the nest of the most sacred of birds?
You and your wife and your palace deserve to be
burnt to ashes!

'But I know this request does not come from you,' the genie continued. 'It comes from the brother of the African magician. He is now in your palace disguised as the holy woman – it was he who put that wish into your wife's head. Take care of yourself, for he means to kill you.' And saying this the genie disappeared.

Aladdin went back to the princess, saying his head ached, and requested that the holy Fatima should be fetched to lay her hands on him. But when the magician's brother came near, Aladdin seized his dagger and pierced him to the heart.

'What have you done?' cried the princess. 'You have killed the holy woman!'

'Not so,' replied Aladdin, and told her of how she had been deceived.

After this Aladdin and his wife lived in peace in their beautiful palace. When the Sultan died, Aladdin took his place and reigned for many years, leaving behind him a long line of just and beloved kings.

THE ENCHANTED HORSE

t was the Feast of the New Year, the oldest and most splendid of all the feasts in the Kingdom of Persia, and the day had been spent by the king in the city of Schiraz, watching all kinds of magnificent shows and sights prepared by his subjects. The sun was setting, and he was about to give his court the signal to retire, when suddenly an Indian appeared before his throne, leading a richly harnessed horse. It was a beautiful life-size model – although in every way it looked exactly like a real creature.

'Sire,' he said humbly, 'although I make my appearance so late before your Highness, I can confidently assure you that none of the wonders you have seen today can be compared to this horse.'

'I see nothing in it,' replied the king. 'It is just a clever imitation of a real one, and any skilled workman might do as much.'

'Sire,' returned the Indian, 'I do not speak about his appearance but of what he can do! I have only to mount him and wish myself in some special place, no matter how distant it may be, and in a very few moments I shall find myself there. It is this, Sire, that makes the horse so marvellous. If your Highness will allow me, I will prove it to you.'

The King of Persia, who was interested in anything unusual and had never before come across such a horse, told the Indian to mount the animal, and show what he could do. In an instant the man leaped onto the horse, and inquired where the king wished to send him.

'Do you see that mountain?' asked the king, point-ing to a huge mass that towered into the sky about three leagues from Schiraz. 'Well, go and bring me the leaf of a palm that grows at the foot.'

The words were hardly out of the king's mouth when the Indian turned a screw placed in the horse's neck, close to the saddle. The animal bounded like lightning up into the air, and was soon beyond the sight even of the sharpest eyes. In a quarter of an hour the Indian returned, bearing in his hand the palm. Guiding his horse to the foot of the throne, he dis-mounted, and laid the leaf before the king.

No sooner had the king seen the astonishing speed of which the horse was capable, than he longed to possess it himself. Indeed, so sure was he that the Indian would be quite ready to sell, that he looked upon it as his own already.

'I never guessed how valuable an animal it was,' he remarked to the Indian, 'and I am grateful to you for having shown me my mistake. If you will sell it to me, how much must I pay you?'

'Sire,' replied the Indian, 'I never doubted that a sovereign so wise as your Highness would do justice to my horse, once he knew of its power. Greatly as I prize it, I will give it up to your Highness, but on one condition. The horse was not constructed by me, but was given to me by the inventor in exchange for my only daughter. I took a solemn oath that I would never part with it, except for some object of equal value.'

'Name anything you like,' cried the king, inter-rupting him. 'My kingdom is large, and filled with fair

cities. You have only to choose which you would prefer, to become its ruler to the end of your life.'

'Sire,' answered the Indian, to whom the proposal did not seem nearly so generous as it appeared to the king, 'I am most grateful to your Highness for your princely offer. I beg you not to be offended if I say that I can only deliver up my horse in exchange for the hand of the princess your daughter.'

A shout of laughter burst from the courtiers as they heard these words, and Prince Firouz, the heir apparent, was filled with anger at the Indian's impudence. The king, however, thought that parting with the princess was not such a great price to pay in order to gain such a delightful toy. But while he was hesitating as to his answer the prince broke in.

'Sire,' he said, 'you cannot doubt for an instant what reply you should give to such an insolent bargain. Consider your honour and that of your ancestors.'

'My son,' replied the king, 'you speak nobly, but you do not realise the value of the horse. And, if I reject his offer, he will only make the same to some other ruler. I should be filled with despair at the thought that anyone but myself should own this Seventh Wonder of the World. I do not say that I shall accept his conditions, but I should like you to examine the horse and, with the owner's permission, to try out its powers.'

The Indian, who had overheard the king's speech, thought it almost certain that his proposals would be accepted, so he joyfully agreed and came forward to help the prince mount the horse and show him how to

guide it. But, before he could finish, the young man had turned the screw and was soon out of sight!

They waited some time, expecting that every moment he might be seen returning in the distance, but at length the Indian grew frightened. Throwing himself down before the throne, he said to the king, 'Sire, your Highness must have noticed that the prince was so impatient I was not able to tell him how to return to the place from which he started. I implore you not to punish me, or to blame me for any misfortune that may occur.'

'But why,' cried the king in a burst of fear and anger, 'why did you not call him back when you saw him disappearing?'

'Sire,' replied the Indian, 'I was so surprised by how quickly he moved that I was speechless! But we must hope that he will find and turn the second screw, which will bring the horse back to earth.'

'But supposing he does!' shouted the king, 'what is to stop the horse from descending straight into the sea, or dashing him to pieces on the rocks?'

'Have no fears, your Highness,' said the Indian, 'the horse has the gift of passing over seas, and of carrying his rider wherever he wishes to go.'

'Well, your head shall answer for it,' returned the king. 'If in three months I have no news that he is safe, I will have you executed!' So saying, he ordered his guards to seize the Indian and throw him into prison.

Meanwhile, Prince Firouz had gone gaily up into the air, and for the space of an hour went higher and higher, until even the tallest mountains were spread out below him. Then he began to think it was time to come down, imagining that all he had to do was to turn the screw the reverse way. But, to his surprise and horror, he found that, however hard he turned, it made not the slightest difference. He then remembered that he had never waited to ask how he was to get back to earth again, and realized he was in grave danger. Luckily, though, the prince did not lose his head, and instead set about examining the horse's head with great care. At last, to his relief, he discovered a tiny little peg, much smaller than the other, close to the right ear. This he turned, and found himself dropping slowly to the earth.

It was now dark and, although the prince was rather worried, he was obliged to let the horse go its own way, as he could see nothing. It was already past midnight when Prince Firouz again touched the ground, faint and weary from his long ride, and from the fact that he had eaten nothing since early morning.

The first thing he did on dismounting was to try to find out where he was. As far as he could discover in the thick darkness, he found himself on a marble terrace – the roof of a huge

palace. In one corner of the terrace stood a small door, opening on to a staircase which led down into the palace.

Some people might have hesitated before exploring further, but not the prince. 'I am doing no harm,' he said to himself, 'and whoever the owner is, he will not touch me when he sees I am unarmed.' So he went cautiously down the staircase. On a landing, he noticed an open door, beyond which was a faintly lit hall.

Before entering, the prince paused and listened, but he heard nothing except the sound of men snoring. By the light of a lantern hanging from the roof, he saw a row of black guards sleeping, each with a naked sword lying by him. He realised that this must be the guard-room outside the chamber of some queen or princess.

Standing quite still, Prince Firouz looked about him, till his eyes grew used to the gloom, and he noticed a bright light shining through a curtain in one corner. He then made his way softly towards it and, drawing aside its folds, passed into a splendid chamber. It was full of women, lying asleep on low couches, except for one who was on a large, magnificent bed. This, he knew, must be the princess.

Gently stealing up to the side of her bed, he looked at her and saw that she was more beautiful than any woman he had ever seen before! The prince was fascinated, but he was also well aware of the danger of his position, as one cry of surprise would awake the guards, and cause his certain death.

So sinking quietly on his knees, he took hold of the

sleeve of the princess and drew her arm lightly towards him. The princess opened her eyes and, seeing before her a handsome well-dressed man, she remained speechless with astonishment.

This favourable moment was seized by the prince who, bowing low, spoke softly to her,

'You behold, madame, a prince in distress, son to the King of Persia, who, owing to an adventure so strange that you will scarcely believe it, finds himself here, humbly begging your protection. Only yesterday, I was in my father's court. Today, I am in an unknown land, in danger of my life.'

N ow the princess was the eldest daughter of the King of Bengal, who was enjoying a peaceful change in her own special palace, which lay a little distance from the capital. She listened kindly to what he had to say, and then answered,

'Prince, do not be uneasy. We in Bengal are just as kind to strangers as you are in Persia. You have my word you will be protected.' And as the prince was about to thank her for her goodness, she added quickly, 'I am curious to learn by what means you have travelled here so speedily, but I know that you must be faint for want of food. I shall give orders to my women to take you to one of my chambers, where you will be given food and left to sleep.'

By this time the princess's attendants were all awake, and listening to the conversation. At a sign from their mistress they rose, dressed themselves hastily and, snatching up some of the candles which lighted the room, conducted the prince to a large and

lofty room. Two of them prepared his bed, and the rest went down to the kitchen, returning with all sorts of dishes. They showed him cupboards filled with clothes and linen, then left the room.

During their absence the Princess of Bengal, who had been greatly struck by the beauty of the prince, tried in vain to go to sleep again. It was of no use – she felt wide awake and, when her women came back, she inquired eagerly if the prince had all he wanted, and what they thought of him.

'Madame,' they replied, 'we cannot tell what impression this young man has made on you. For ourselves, we think you would be very lucky if your father allowed you to marry anyone so pleasing. Certainly there is no one in the Court of Bengal who can be compared with him.'

The princess was secretly pleased at this but, as she did not wish to betray her own feelings, she merely said, 'You are all a set of chatterboxes; go back to bed, and let me sleep.'

When she dressed the following morning, her maids noticed that the princess was very particular, and insisted on her hair being dressed two or three times over. 'For,' she said to herself, 'if the prince liked me when I looked so ordinary last night, just think how much more will he be struck with me when he sees me beautifully dressed.'

Then she placed in her hair the largest and most brilliant diamonds she could find, and donned a necklace, bracelets and girdle all of precious stones. Over

her shoulders her ladies put a robe of the richest fabric in all the Indies, that no one was allowed to wear except members of the royal family. When she was fully dressed, she sent a messenger ahead to wake the prince so he would be ready to receive her.

In a few moments the princess herself appeared and, after the usual compliments had passed between them, the princess sat down on a sofa. 'I could not receive you in my own apartments,' she explained, 'because we might have been interrupted at any hour by the chief of the guards. He has the right to enter whenever it pleases him, whereas this chamber is forbidden ground and we will not be disturbed. I am so impatient to hear about the wonderful accident which has brought you here, so do begin, I beg you.'

So the prince explained all about the enchanted horse which had been brought to his father, and of the absurd price the Indian had asked for it – the hand of the princess his sister! 'But though all the bystanders laughed and mocked, and I was beside myself with rage, I saw to my despair that my father was sorely tempted – he wished so strongly to own the horse. He begged me to look at it more closely, so I mounted and turned the peg as I had seen the Indian do. In an instant I was soaring upwards, much quicker than an arrow could fly, and I felt as if I was so near the sky that I should soon hit my head against it! I could see nothing beneath me, and for some time was so confused that I did not even know in what direction I was travelling. At last when it was growing dark, I found another screw, and on

turning it, the horse began slowly to sink towards the earth.

'Fate led me to land here, in your kingdom, and the rest, Princess, you know. It only remains for me to thank you for the kindness you have shown me, and to assure you of my gratitude. By the law of nations, I am already your slave, and I have only my heart that is my own, to offer you. Madame, it was yours from the first moment I beheld you!'

The princess blushed prettily and for a moment was so confused she couldn't speak.

'Prince,' she said finally, 'I bless the chance which led you here. You could have entered no house which would have given you a warmer welcome. As to your being a slave, be assured that you are as free here as at your father's court. As to your heart,' continued she in tones of encouragement, 'I am quite sure *that* must have been disposed of long ago, to some princess who is well worthy of it.'

Prince Firouz was about to protest that there was no lady with any prior claims, when one of the princess's attendants entered and announced that dinner was served.

D inner was laid in a magnificent apartment. The table was covered with delicious fruits and richly dressed girls sang softly and sweetly to the accompaniment of stringed instruments while the prince and princess ate. Then, when they had finished, they passed into a small room hung with blue and gold, looking out into a garden. It was filled with exotic trees and flowers, the like of which the prince

had never seen in Persia.

The princess, seeing that he was impressed, said, 'I assure you my father's palace and gardens are even more beautiful. I hope you will agree to visit him there soon.'

Now the princess hoped that, by bringing about a meeting between the prince and her father, the King would be so struck with the young man's distinguished air and fine manners, that he would offer him his daughter's hand in marriage. But the reply of the Prince of Persia was not quite what she wished.

'Madame,' he said, 'I cannot possibly present myself before so great a sovereign without the attendants suitable to my rank. He would think me a mere adventurer.'

'If that is all,' she answered, 'you can get as many attendants here as you please. There are plenty of Persian merchants and, as for money, my treasury is always open to you. Take what you please.'

rince Firouz realized the princess must care for him very much, but although his passion for her increased with every moment, he did not forget his duty. 'I do not know, Princess, how to express my gratitude, but the King my father must be worried about my disappearance. I should be unworthy of all the love he showers upon me if I did

not return to him at the first possible moment. While I am enjoying myself with a beautiful princess, I fear that he is plunged in the deepest grief, having lost all hope of seeing me again. So I am sure you will understand why I must return. But I shall count the moments when, with your gracious permission, I may present myself before the King of Bengal, not as a wanderer, but as a prince, to implore the favour of your hand.'

The Princess of Bengal was too reasonable not to accept this, but she was afraid that if the prince left straight away the impression she had made on him would fade away. So she made one more effort to keep him, and begged him to give her just a day or two more of his company.

I n common politeness the prince could hardly refuse this request, and the princess set about inventing every kind of amusement for him. She succeeded so well that not two days, but two months, slipped by almost unnoticed – in balls, spectacles and in hunting. But at last, one day, the prince declared seriously that he could neglect his duty no longer, and entreated her to put no further obstacles in his way. He promised to return, as soon as he could. But as he was about to leave, the prince had an idea.

'Princess,' he said, 'I am no false lover whose devotion cannot stand the test of absence. But I beseech you to come with me, for my life can only be happy when passed with you, and you will be warmly welcomed in Persia.'

The princess was at first afraid that Prince Firouz did not know how to manage the horse, and she dreaded lest they find themselves in the same plight as before. But the prince soothed her fears so successfully that soon she had no other thought than to arrange for their flight so secretly that no one in the palace should suspect it.

Early the following morning, when the whole palace was wrapped in sleep, she stole up on to the roof. There, the prince was already awaiting her, with his horse's head towards Persia. He mounted first, and helped the princess up behind. Then, when she was firmly seated, with her hands holding tightly to his belt, he touched the screw and the horse began to leave the earth quickly behind him.

He travelled just as swiftly as before, and Prince Firouz guided him so well that in two and a half hours from the time of starting, he saw the capital of Persia lying beneath him. He decided to land neither in the great square from which he had started, nor in the Sultan's palace, but in a country house at a little distance from the town. Here he showed the princess a beautiful suite of rooms, and begged her to rest, while he informed his father of their arrival and prepared a public reception worthy of her rank. Then he ordered a horse to be saddled and set out.

All the way through the streets he was welcomed with shouts of joy by the people, who had long lost all hope of seeing him again. On reaching the palace, he found the Sultan surrounded by his

ministers, all clad in the deepest mourning. His father almost went out of his mind with surprise and delight at the sight of his son and, when he had calmed down a little, he begged the prince to relate his adventures.

The prince at once told him all about the Princess of Bengal, not even concealing the fact that she had fallen in love with him. 'And, Sire,' ended the prince, 'having given my royal word that you would consent to our marriage, I persuaded her to return with me on the Indian's horse. I have left her in one of your Highness's country houses, where she is waiting now.'

As he said this the prince was about to throw himself at the feet of the Sultan to beg his permission to marry, but his father prevented him and, embracing him again, said eagerly:

'My son, not only do I gladly consent to your marriage with the Princess of Bengal, but I will hasten to pay my respects to her, and to thank her myself for everything she has done for you. I will then bring her back with me, and make all arrangements for the wedding to be celebrated today.'

So the Sultan gave orders that the people should throw off their mourning, and that there should be a concert of drums, trumpets and cymbals. He also remembered the Indian, and demanded that he should be brought before him.

The Indian was led into his presence, surrounded by guards. 'I have kept you locked up,' said the Sultan, 'so that in case my son was lost, your life should pay the penalty. He has now returned, so take your horse, and be gone for ever.'

The Indian hastily left the Sultan, full of anger at the treatment he had received. When he was outside, he inquired of the prison guards where the prince had really been all this time, and what he had been doing. They told him the whole story, and how the Princess of Bengal was even then waiting in the country palace for the Sultan to give his consent for their marriage.

At once the Indian decided on a plan of revenge. Going straight to the country house, he informed the doorkeeper that he had been sent by the Sultan and by the Prince of Persia to fetch the princess on the enchanted horse, and to bring her to the palace.

The doorkeeper suspected nothing, and straight away led him to the Princess of Bengal. She, too, saw nothing to fear in his proposal and gladly consented to do what he wished.

The Indian, delighted with the success of his scheme, mounted the horse, helped the princess up behind him, and turned the peg. It was the very moment that the prince was leaving the palace, followed closely by the Sultan and all the Court. So the Indian steered the horse right above them, knowing that then they could not help but see his sweet revenge!

When the Sultan of Persia saw the horse and its riders, he stopped short with astonishment and horror, and broke out into oaths and curses. The Indian was unmoved, knowing that he was perfectly safe from pursuit.

But furious as the Sultan was, his feelings were nothing to those of Prince Firouz when he saw his

beloved princess being carried rapidly away. And while he was struck speechless with grief she vanished swiftly out of his sight.

What was he to do? Gathering together all his love and his courage, he continued on his way to the palace, thinking all the time of what he could do. There, the doorkeeper flung himself at his master's feet, imploring his pardon. 'Rise,' said the prince, 'I am the cause of this misfortune, not you. But if you want to help me, go and find the robe of a monk, but beware of saying it is for me.'

The doorkeeper managed to do just this, and the prince immediately put on the robe instead of his own. He had decided to venture forth in disguise to search for the princess throughout the land. He left the house at nightfall, uncertain where to start looking, but firmly resolved not to return without his true love.

M eanwhile the Indian directed the horse towards a wood close to the capital of the kingdom of Cashmere. Feeling very hungry, and supposing that the princess also might be in want of food, he brought his steed down to the earth, and left the princess in a shady place on the banks of a clear stream.

At first, when the princess found herself alone, she thought about trying to escape and hide. But as she had eaten scarcely anything since she had left Bengal, she felt she was too weak to go far. When the

Indian returned with meats of various kinds, she ate ravenously and soon felt strong again. Then the Indian taunted her with insolent remarks, and she sprang to her feet, calling loudly for help! Luckily her cries were heard by a troop of horsemen, who rode up to inquire what was the matter.

Now the leader of these horsemen was the Sultan of Cashmere, returning from a hunt, and he instantly turned to the Indian to ask who this lady was. The Indian rudely answered that it was his wife, and there was no need for anyone else to interfere.

'My lord,' cried the Princess, 'whoever you may be, put no faith in this imposter. He is an abominable magician, who has this day torn me from the Prince of Persia, my destined husband, and brought me here on this enchanted horse.' She would have continued, but her tears choked her. And the Sultan of Cashmere, convinced by her beauty and her distinguished air that the tale was true, ordered his followers to cut off the Indian's head and take the enchanted horse to his palace.

The princess had been rescued from one peril, but it seemed as if she had only fallen into another. The Sultan commanded a horse to be given her, and conducted her to his own palace, where he led her to a beautiful apartment and surrounded her with slave girls and guards. Then, without allowing her time to thank him for all he had done, he told her to rest, saying she should tell him her adventures on the following day.

The princess fell asleep, flattering herself that she had only to relate her story for the Sultan to be touched by compassion, and to restore her to the prince without delay. But a few hours later her hopes were dashed!

When the Sultan of Cashmere had left the princess, he had resolved that the sun should not set again without her becoming his wife. At daybreak he proclaimed the marriage throughout the town, and the sound of drums, trumpets, cymbals, and other instruments filled the air. The Princess of Bengal was awakened early by the noise, but she did not for one moment imagine that it had anything to do with her. Then the Sultan arrived to inform her that the trumpet blasts she heard were part of their solemn marriage ceremonies! This unexpected announcement caused the princess such terror that she sank down in a dead faint.

The slaves that were in waiting ran to her aid, and the Sultan himself did his best to bring her back to consciousness. At length her senses began slowly to come back to her. But when she remembered her plight she decided that, rather than break faith with the Prince of Persia by consenting to such a marriage, she would pretend she was mad. So she began by saying all sorts of absurd things, and using all kinds of strange gestures, while the Sultan stood watching her with sorrow and surprise. He left her to her women, ordering them to take the greatest care of her. But as the day went on, the violent madness seemed to become worse.

Days passed in this manner, till at last the Sultan of Cashmere decided to summon all the doctors of his court to consult together over her sad state. Their answer was that madness is of so many different kinds that it was impossible to give an opinion on the case without seeing the princess. So the Sultan gave orders that they were to be introduced into her chamber, one by one, every man according to his rank.

The princess knew she had to do everything in her power to stop the doctors examining her closely, for even the most ignorant of them would soon discover that she was in perfectly good health. So, as each man approached, she broke out into such violent fits that not one dared to lay a finger on her. A few, who pretended to be cleverer than the rest, declared that they could diagnose her sickness merely by looking at her and ordered her certain potions. The princess took them all without worrying, for she knew they could not 'cure' her!

When the Sultan of Cashmere saw that the court doctors could no nothing to cure the princess, he called in those from the city and all the largest towns, who fared no better. Finding that the task was beyond them, he finally sent messengers into the other neighbouring states, offering to pay the expenses of any doctor who would come and see the princess, and a handsome reward to the one who could cure her.

In answer to this proclamation many foreign professors flocked into Cashmere, but of course they were no more successful than the rest had been, as the cure depended only on the princess herself.

I t was during this time that Prince Firouz, still in
disguise as a humble monk, wandering sadly and
hopelessly from place to place, arrived in a large
city of India. There he heard a great deal of talk about
a Princess of Bengal who had gone out of her senses,
on the very day that she was to have been married to
the Sultan of Cashmere. This was quite enough to
make him take the road to Cashmere to find out the
whole story. When he knew that he had at last found
the princess whom he had been looking for for so
long, he immediately set about devising a plan for
her rescue.

The first thing he did was to borrow a doctor's robe.
With the long beard he had grown on his travels, he
looked just right for the part. He then lost no time in
going to the palace, where he saw the chief minister.
He apologised for his boldness in believing he could
cure the princess where so many others had failed,
but he explained he had some secret remedies which
had always succeeded in such cases before.

The minister assured him that he was heartily welcome, and that he would gain a magnificent reward if
he succeeded. The Sultan wasted no time in talking.
He led the prince up to a room under the roof which
had an opening through which he could observe the
princess, without himself being seen.

The prince looked, and beheld the princess re-
clining on a sofa with tears in her eyes. She was
singing softly a song bewailing her sad destiny which
had deprived her, perhaps for ever, of the man she so
tenderly loved. The young man's heart beat fast as
he listened, for he needed no further proof that her

madness was merely an act, and that it was love of him which had caused her to resort to this trick.

He softly left his hiding-place and returned to the Sultan, reporting that he was sure from certain signs that the princess's illness was not incurable, but that he must see her and speak with her alone.

The Sultan made no objection, and commanded that the prince should be taken to the princess's apartment. The moment she caught sight of his doctor's robe, she sprang from her seat in a fury, and heaped insults upon him. The prince took no notice of her behaviour and, approaching quite close so that his words might be heard by her alone, he said in a low whisper, 'Look at me, Princess, and you will see that I am no doctor, but the Prince of Persia, who has come to set you free.'

t the sound of his voice, the Princess of Bengal suddenly grew calm, and an expression of joy spread over her face, such as only comes when what we wish for most, and expect the least, suddenly happens. For some time she was too enchanted to speak, and Prince Firouz took advantage of her silence to explain to her all that had occurred – his despair at watching her disappear before his very eyes, the oath he had sworn to follow her over the world, and his joy at finally discovering her in the palace at Cashmere. When he had finished, he begged the princess to tell him how she had come to the palace so that he might work out a plan to rescue her from the tyranny of the Sultan.

It took no time at all for the princess to explain how she had been forced to play the part of a mad woman, in order to escape a marriage with the Sultan to which he hadn't even asked her consent!

Neither of them knew where the enchanted horse could be found, although they thought the Sultan must be keeping it safely somewhere. But, in spite of this, soon they had made their plans to escape.

The next morning – and the next – the princess dressed with care and received the Sultan gracefully. He was delighted, quite sure that a complete cure was taking place. Meanwhile the 'doctor' humbly inquired by what means the Princess of Bengal had reached Cashmere, which was so far distant from her father's kingdom, and how she came to be there alone. The Sultan thought the question very natural, and told him the same story that the Princess of Bengal had done, adding that he had ordered the enchanted horse to be taken to his treasury as a curiosity, though he was quite ignorant how it could be used.

'Sire,' replied the doctor, 'your Highness's tale has supplied me with the clue I needed to complete the recovery of the princess. During her voyage on the enchanted horse, part of its magic has been transferred to her person. It can only be banished with certain secret perfumes I possess. Command the horse to be brought into the big square outside the palace, and leave the rest to me. I promise that in a very few moments, in presence of all the court and people, you shall see the princess as healthy both in mind and body as ever she was in her life. And in order to make the spectacle as impressive as possible, I would

suggest that she should be richly dressed and covered with the noblest jewels of the crown.'

The Sultan readily agreed to all that the prince proposed – the following morning the enchanted horse should be taken from the treasury, and brought into the great square of the palace. Soon the rumour began to spread through the town that something extraordinary was about to happen, and such a crowd began to collect that the guards had to be called out to keep order, and to make way for the enchanted horse.

When all was ready, the Sultan appeared, and took his place on a platform, surrounded by the chief nobles and officers of his court. When they were seated, the Princess of Bengal emerged from the palace, accompanied by the ladies who had been given to her by the Sultan. She slowly approached the enchanted horse and, with the help of her ladies, got up on to its back.

Directly she was in the saddle, with her feet in the stirrups and the bridle in her hand, the prince placed around the horse six iron baskets full of burning coals, into each of which he threw a perfume composed of all sorts of delicious scents. Then he crossed his

hands over his breast, and with lowered eyes walked three times round the horse, muttering some 'magic' words. Soon there arose from the burning braziers a thick smoke which almost hid both the horse and the princess. This was the moment for which he had been waiting!

Springing lightly up behind his lady, the prince leaned forward and turned the peg and, as the horse darted up into the air, he cried aloud so that his words were heard by all present,

'Sultan of Cashmere, when you wish to marry princesses who have sought your protection, learn first to gain their consent!'

I t was in this way that the Prince of Persia rescued the Princess of Bengal, and returned with her to Persia, where they came to land this time before the palace of the King himself. Their marriage was delayed just long enough to make the ceremony as brilliant as possible. And as soon as the rejoicings were over, an ambassador was sent to the King of Bengal, to inform him of what had passed, and to ask his blessing on the alliance between the two countries, which he heartily gave.

After this, the prince and princess lived happily in their own beautiful palace and kept the enchanted horse in pride of place to remind them ever more of their strange adventure.